QUARRY IN THE MIDDLE

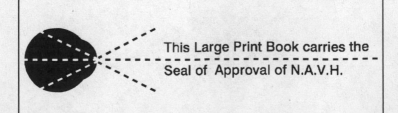

This Large Print Book carries the
Seal of Approval of N.A.V.H.

QUARRY IN THE MIDDLE

MAX ALLAN COLLINS

THORNDIKE PRESS
A part of Gale, Cengage Learning

GALE
CENGAGE Learning™

Detroit • New York • San Francisco • New Haven, Conn • Waterville, Maine • London

Copyright © 2009 by Max Allan Collins.

The name "Hard Case Crime" and the Hard Case Crime logo are trademarks of Winterfall LLC. Hard Case Crime books are selected and edited by Charles Ardai.

Thorndike Press, a part of Gale, Cengage Learning.

Thorndike Press® Large Print Mystery.

The text of this Large Print edition is unabridged.

Other aspects of the book may vary from the original edition.

Set in 16 pt. Plantin.

Printed on permanent paper.

LIBRARY OF CONGRESS CATALOGING-IN-PUBLICATION DATA

Collins, Max Allan.
   Quarry in the middle / by Max Allan Collins. — Large print ed.
      p. cm. — (Thorndike Press large print mystery)
     Originally published: New York : Hard Case Crime, 2009.
     ISBN-13: 978-1-4104-2485-3 (alk. paper)
     ISBN-10: 1-4104-2485-5 (alk. paper)
     1. Murder for hire—Fiction. 2. Organized crime—Fiction. 3. Large type books. I. Title.
   PS3553.O4753Q37 2010
   813'.54—dc22   2009049414

Published in 2010 by arrangement with Hard Case Crime and Leisure Books, a division of Dorchester Publishing Co., Inc.

For Richard Stark

"Feed lettuce to the bunny and eat the bunny."

DASHIELL HAMMETT

"In a mad world, only the mad are sane."

AKIRA KUROSAWA

"An assassin can display a sublime altruism."

SERGIO LEONE

ONE

I had a body in the trunk of my car.

I hadn't planned it that way, but then it wasn't that kind of job. It wasn't a job at all, really, rather a speculative venture, and now I'd made more of an investment than just my time and a little money.

This was in the summer, and Reagan was still president, early enough that he wasn't showing his Alzheimer's yet and late enough that he was keeping a good distance between himself and the Press Corps, waving and smiling and pretending he couldn't hear them. We'd already had the Chernobyl meltdown, the *Challenger* explosion, and Pac-Man fever. Disco was dead, which was fine with me, only I wish somebody had paid me to kill the fucker.

I make the above lame joke because I had once upon a time killed people for money — initially for Uncle Sam, but more profitably for a mobbed-up guy called the Broker

9

(more about him later). Right now I was in business for myself, thirty-five years old and looking to make a killing. Financial kind.

Anyway, the body in the trunk of my car. And it *was* my car, not a rental, a blue '75 Pontiac with a lighter blue vinyl top, a Sunbird, which was really just a Vega pretending to be a sports car. It had a lot of miles on it and had only cost a grand and change, bought for cash under a phony name in Wisconsin — another investment in this spec job.

I hadn't known I'd wind up with a body in the trunk, but I was old enough a hand at this to know I didn't want to use my usual vehicle and a rental would be a bad idea, too. But to tell you the truth, I'd had bodies in my trunk before, so maybe that was a factor, after all.

For around six years in the '70s I had taken on contracts, and part of why I'd survived and even flourished was my ability to blend in. At five ten, one-hundred-sixty pounds, I'd maintained a fairly boyish look — into my late twenties, I could be been taken for a college student, and now I could pass for twenty-five or -six. I kept my brown hair medium-length because that helped maintain anonymity. I could be a working man in t-shirt and jeans or a salesman in narrow tie and sportcoat or a professional in button-down collar and pinstripe suit.

Tonight, though, I was doing my Don Johnson impression in a white Armani suit with a pastel yellow t-shirt and Italian loafers with no socks. Normally, the *Miami Vice* schtick was not for me, but I needed to fit in. The Paddlewheel attracted a wealthy crowd, and the over-forty set dressed to the nines, but the twenty-and thirty-somethings were Yuppies and dressed accordingly.

So tonight I was a Yuppie (a Yuppie with a body in the trunk, but a Yuppie).

This was a warm evening cooled by a breeze and the parking lot was nearly full — my used car at least had that vinyl top to help it fit in with the Buicks and Caddies and BMW's, and was maybe sporty enough to cohabit with the Stingray 280ZX's and Jags. I parked on the far side of the lot, near where the glimmering black strip of the Mississippi River reflected the lights of the ancient steel toll bridge joining River's Bluff, Iowa, and Haydee's Port, Illinois.

Everybody I'd talked to so far, which wasn't many admittedly, seemed to shorten it to Haydee's. And from the glimpse I'd got of the little town, they might have been saying Hades, and meaning it.

River's Bluff itself hadn't been that impressive, a long-in-the-tooth industrial burg of maybe sixty thousand on rolling hills overlooking the river. Ivy-covered shelves of shale lined the freeway cutting through the old river city, taking me to the bridge and a thirty-cent toll. Going over the rumbling, ancient span was a more frightening ride than a fifty-cent one at any carnival.

And Haydee's Port itself wasn't any less frightening. A sign beyond the bridge announced it, a road curving right to eventually deposit me and my Sunbird (no body in the trunk yet — this was early afternoon) in a pocket below the interstate. Here I found myself beholding the open wound that was Haydee's Port.

Main Street was almost entirely bars and strip clubs, rough-looking ones — big parking lots in back, empty mid-morning but indicating healthy-sized clientele. Among the few respectable businesses was a Casey's General Store, which was also the only gas station, on a corner by itself just beyond the two-block strip of sin. No schools, and certainly no churches. Poking up out of the trees that hugged the Mighty Miss emerged grain-elevator towers, which were one legitimate business anyway that had nothing to do with selling beer, except maybe providing out-of-state brewers with some of

12

the makings.

Main Street was paved, but the others weren't, just narrow hard dirt, with ruts to indicate what happened when it rained. The main drag was built with its back to the river, putting the residences of the little community behind the opposite row of saloons. Mostly Haydee's Port was a glorified trailer park, minus the glory — shabby mobile homes here and there, as if where the most recent tornado had left them, with an occasional sagging twenties or older vintage clapboard house to add a little undignified variety.

This was a welfare ghetto, with the bars handy for disposal of monthly checks and probably willing to accept food stamps, maybe at 75 cents on the dollar.

All of which made the Paddlewheel (half a mile or so out of town) such an anomaly, at least at first glance. This was a class operation, not an all-night gin mill serving blue-collar out-of-workers or the spillover from River Bluff after the bars closed, rather a high-end entertainment complex that attracted clientele with cash, not food stamps. The reconverted warehouse was a massive affair, home to a restaurant, numerous bars, several lounges with stages, and a casino — a mini-Las Vegas under one roof.

Though when you really thought about it, the Paddlewheel was not an anomaly at all — some genius entrepreneur had realized that in an environment corrupt enough for downtown Haydee's Port to openly thrive, erecting a sin palace for Mr. and Mrs. Gotrocks Midwest was also possible. Whatever bent cops and greedy politicos were allowing these lowlife joints to run wide open would be just as for sale to the Paddlewheel's backers. Maybe more so.

Anyway, the body in the trunk.

You have to understand that I had no idea I was heading for Haydee's Port. Hell, I had no idea Haydee's Port existed. I'd been following a guy named Monahan from Omaha, Nebraska, which had been tricky for a variety of reasons, starting with the difficulty of staking out a guy who lives in a suburban home in an upper middle-class neighborhood.

Monahan was a guy about about forty who lived a very respectable life for a contract killer, which is what he was. He was five seven or eight, in good shape, with short dark hair and the general button-down look of an insurance salesman, which as it happened was his cover.

I had no reason to believe his perky little blonde wife, also about forty, had the faint-

14

est notion Monahan was a hit man, to use the TV parlance. Certainly his two kids, a boy around thirteen and a girl of fifteen or sixteen were clueless that their suburban lifestyle was made possible by the man of the house committing commercial carnage.

Monahan's life with his wife and kids and his split-level in a housing development in Omaha have almost nothing to do with this narrative, so I'll keep it short. I'd never met him, but he was one of fifty-some guys like me who had worked for the Broker, the middleman who'd provided me with contracts back when I was in the killing game myself. For reasons recorded elsewhere, the Broker wound up dead and I wound up with a database of his worker bees.

"Database" isn't exactly right, because when I came into possession of that file, it was before home computers, and when I say "file," I mean literally that — a file, a fat manila folder full of extensive information including real names and aliases alike, addresses past and present, photographs for each name, even specific jobs that had been carried out.

Why the Broker maintained this explosive packet, I couldn't say — eventual blackmail purposes should someone get out of line, maybe? Or food for the feds or cops should immunity and the Witness Protection Program come into play?

For all his veneer of suburban bliss, Monahan was an assassin whose specialty was particularly nasty: hit-and-run kills. This had made him one of the highest paid names on the Broker's list — Monahan provided the kind of accidental death that sent official investigations off on the wrong track, and made handsome insurance payouts a breeze. As a professional, the guy had real skills, and you had to hand it to him.

But as I believe I already indicated, maintaining surveillance on a guy living in a housing development is a royal pain in the ass. Luckily I was able to rent a house just down the street from him on the opposite side of the block. I spent my time tailing him to the office he maintained in a strip mall, where he read newspapers and watched television and boinked a Chinese girl who worked for the carry-out joint two doors down; sometimes he went home on the lunch hour and boinked his cute wife, too. You know what they say about boinking Chinese girls — an hour later, you're horny again.

So I smiled at my neighbors and mowed my fucking lawn and attended junior high baseball games and a jazz dance recital (the fifteen year-old blonde daughter looked good in a leotard) and even saw a *Beverly Hills Cop* movie and generally kept track of the prick.

Here's the thing — after the Broker bought it, I decided I'd never work for a middleman again. Broker had betrayed me, and seeing his file with my own mug in it with detailed info about two dozen kills I'd been in on made me, let's say, less than eager to ever work for anybody who wasn't me. Pretty soon I'd figured out a way to use the file to stay in the same game, but on my own terms.

I would choose a name from the Broker's list — the name of someone like myself — and go and stake out that party, then follow him or her to their next gig. Once I figured out who the hitter's target was, I would approach said target and let him or her know he or she was in somebody's fucking crosshairs.

I'd offer to discreetly eliminate the hired killer (sometimes, killers) for a fee that was in no way nominal. Further, I'd offer to look into who had hired the hit, and remove them, for the kind of bonus that meant I wouldn't have to do this more than once a year or so.

You might find this risky — what if the

target freaked out, being approached by a stranger with a wild story, a stranger who claims to be a kind of professional killer himself, and called the cops or otherwise went apeshit. But the thing is, anyone who has been designated for a hit is somebody who almost certainly has done something worth getting killed over. These tend not to be shining, solid citizens. You don't inspire somebody to kill your ass by behaving yourself.

This is, incidentally, why somebody like me — a guy who is no more twisted than you or your brother or sister or wife — is able to commit murder for money, and sleep just fine. It's down to this: anybody targeted for a hit is somebody who is already dead. They have done something or some things that have made them eligible for being on the wrong end of a bullet or a speeding car or what-have-you, and they are due to die for it. Yes, they are still up and walking around, but that's just a temporary technicality. They are dead already. Obits waiting to be written.

Back when I was doing hits, I was no more unethical than any guy working for a collection agency. I just collected a different kind of payment due. A repo man after something other than appliances, boats or cars.

No denying, though, that murder is illegal and if you're caught doing or having done it, you can earn a cell or a rope or a firing squad or a gas pellet. That meant that the other "collection agency guys" I was now turning the tables on were just as dead as any other designated target.

Anyway, it had mostly worked out well so far — I'd used the Broker's list and taken this approach ten times with occasional glitches but enough success that I was still above ground and with a healthy bank balance to boot.

The downside of my innovative business plan had always been two unpredictable factors. . . .

First, standard operation procedure for hired killings, at least among Broker's crew, meant a two-person team — Passive and Active.

Passive Guy went in to watch the target for at least a week and sometimes up to a month, getting the patterns down. Active Guy would come in a couple days before the hit and get filled in by the Passive partner, often doing his own short-term surveillance to get a feel for what he's up against.

I'd been paired with a number of guys, and usually worked the Active side. I preferred it, but the Broker had insisted I work surveillance one out of four jobs, saying both guys on a team needed to keep their hand in on both roles.

My current approach meant that not only did I have to perform my own surveillance, I had to do so with no knowledge of when my subject's next hit would go down. It was entirely open-ended, and a guy as specialized (and well-paid) as Monahan might only do three or four jobs in a given year.

Meaning I could grin at neighbors, cut grass, watch junior high sports, grow hard-ons over teenage girls in leotards, and take in lousy Eddie Murphy movies for months on end before the real action kicked in.

But this time I got lucky. I only did Suburban Male duty for a little over two weeks before I was on the road, following Monahan to Fuck Knew Where.

Not that this wasn't also tricky — a lot of the driving was on godforsaken flat heartland interstate that made tailing a guy no more obvious than walking into a restaurant with no shoes and no shirt and no pants, either. Luckily turn-offs and rest stops were rare, and I could lay back ten or even twenty miles, and still stay with him.

So this afternoon, Monahan had led me to Haydee's Port, and I had trailed him to the Wheelhouse Motel, which was just outside the cruddy little town, on a curve before you got to the Paddlewheel.

There was nothing cruddy about the Wheelhouse Motel, though, which boasted outdoor pool and satellite TV and a 24-hour truck-stop type restaurant, although there were no gas pumps. I didn't know it yet, but this was the Paddlewheel's official lodgings. The only other motel in town was the Eezer Inn, a dump used for sleeping it off or getting it on, or combinations thereof.

The motel office and the attached restaurant faced the highway and the rooms were along either side of the long, wide structure, with an additional wing down at the end making a right angle beyond the pool. Monahan pulled in on the right and drove down to the last unit of the wing.

I pulled the Sunbird into a spot for restaurant patrons and went in. The place had a three-sided counter and booths along the windows; riverboat prints rode the rough-wood walls, and a big brown metal jukebox squatted near the entryway, with "Proud Mary" playing (the Creedence version).

A booth was waiting from which I could see the unit (Number 36) where Monahan's green Buick Regal was pulled into the adjacent space. The Buick was a car he'd

21

bought in Des Moines, by the way, leaving his own Oldsmobile Cutlass in long-term parking at the airport, though he hadn't been flying anywhere.

I had a good view of that unit, and staring out the window wasn't suspicious, because some good-looking women in their early twenties and skimpy bikinis were using the diving board and splashing around in the pool when they weren't sunning themselves.

I hadn't eaten for a while, so I ordered a Diet Coke and the Famous Wheelhouse Bacon Cheeseburger, which somehow I'd managed never to hear of. Just didn't get around enough, I guess. The famous burger came with fries, which were worthy of fame, because they were hand-cut, not frozen.

These I fearlessly salted and dragged through ketchup and nibbled while I watched the unit; Dionne Warwick was singing "That's What Friends Are For." I'd felt lucky getting hand-cut french fries, but I got luckier yet: Monahan and a skinny blond kid I didn't recognize (not a face in the Broker's file, new blood) exited the motel room and they were walking and talking, casually, and heading my way.

Actually, the restaurant's way. The place had enough patrons to make me inconspicuous, and when Monahan and the blond kid

22

took a booth at the back, against the wall, where I had a good view of them, I managed not to smile.

I say the blond was a kid, but he could have been thirty. He had that blue-eyed Beach Boy look that makes you a kid your whole life (as long as you don't get a gut), including shaggy soup-bowl hair and a tan that said he probably operated out of somewhere coastal. He was wearing a black *Poison* t-shirt with a skull and crossed guitars, so he was a metal head, despite his Mike Love demeanor.

In his short-sleeve light blue shirt with darker blue tie and navy polyester slacks, Monahan looked like the kid's high school counselor. Or he would have if they both hadn't been smoking. Christ, didn't those two know that shit could kill you?

The hardest part was not staring, because they were close enough to lip read. Though surveillance had never been my specialty, I'd done enough of it to pick up the skill in a rudimentary way. What follows is part guess, but it'll give you what I got out of it.

"Sunup," Monahan said.

"Little soon, isn't it?" the blond said, frowning.

"Sooner the better. This is too wide-open here."

"The road?"

"No, the town. You can't predict jack shit in a place like this."

True, I thought, gaining respect for him. *Smart.*

"And too *small,*" the older man went on. "Where do you fuckin' lay low? I don't know how in hell you ain't been spotted."

I wondered if Monahan was one of these guys who reverted to tough-guy talk on the job. Surely he didn't talk like that pretending to be an insurance salesman. I lost respect for him.

"No problems," the kid was saying, grinning, waving it off. "I got a good set-up — farmhouse right across the way."

I'm guessing about "the way," because a waitress in a white-trimmed brown uniform got between us, taking their order.

So I watched the bikini girls for a while. Shit, there were eight or nine of the little dolls frolicking around. Must not have been much to do in Haydee's Port before nightfall.

The waitress left, and the kid asked: "So, first thing, then? *Where,* do you think?"

Monahan's response seemed a non-sequitur: "Only three minutes from that joint to the Interstate ramp."

"That's good." The kid was grinning

24

again. "Perfect from where I'm sittin'."

They stopped talking about the job. Monahan asked the kid about how Heather was doing, and she was doing fine, and this line of lip flap seemed to be about the kid's girl or maybe wife. That meant these two worked together all the time. Not uncommon.

Then their food came, and I let them eat it. I was done with my Famous Bacon Cheeseburger and lesser known fries, and paid at the counter and got the fuck out. I had an idea I knew what they'd been talking about, but I wanted to check it out.

Without even speeding, it was almost exactly three minutes from the Paddlewheel parking lot to the Interstate bridge ramp. I pulled into the restaurant/casino's lot — it was blacktop and half the size of a football field, rows and rows of white-outlined parking spaces. The entrance was near the building, the exit all the way down — only that one way in and one way out. Just seeing the geography told me how Monahan would do it.

Across from the Paddlewheel was a field of corn that wasn't as high as an elephant's eye, but this was only June. A metal gate was across a gravel driveway that angled up to a rundown farmhouse in a small oasis of

25

overgrown grass in the middle of all that corn.

I drove half a mile south and pulled my Sunbird into an access inlet, which enabled tractors and other big farm rigs to get in and out of the cornfield, with the added benefit of slowing down traffic. This time of year nobody was planting or harvesting and I could leave the car there.

The sun hadn't gone down, the temp about eighty-five, so my dark-blue windbreaker wasn't really necessary, and yet it was, because I had my nine millimeter Browning in my waistband and the windbreaker covered it. I was otherwise in black jeans, a light blue Ralph Lauren t-shirt and black running shoes.

Weather aside, the windbreaker also proved invaluable in moving through that cornfield. The blades of those fucking stalks were like nature's razors, and I was glad my head was above them, albeit *just* above. I was headed for that ramshackle two-story farmhouse.

Which, when I got there, showed no signs of life. I could see from some oil on the gravel where the drive came around back that the blond kid (or somebody, but likely the blond kid) had been parking here. He would still be over at the motel for now, though he'd long since finished his own Famous Bacon Cheeseburger and there was no telling at what point he'd return.

That was assuming, of course, that I'd figured right, and that this was where he'd been keeping watch on the target, who was clearly somebody who worked at (or more likely *ran*) the Paddlewheel.

Anyway, I needed to get inside but not in a way the kid would notice. He'd have been going in the back way, but that door, which was up a few paint-peeling wooden steps to the kitchen, was locked. I'd have been surprised to find otherwise.

What did surprise me was how sloppy the kid was — though the same could be true for whatever real estate agency represented the property — as I discovered the slanted cellar doors unlocked. I went down in and found sunlight sneaking in stubby windows onto a mostly empty cement area with a broken-down washer and dryer and not much else but exposed beams. There were pools of moisture here and there, but I could skirt them. I heard some mice or rats scurry, but they stayed out of my way and I did them the same favor.

The chance of anybody being upstairs was minimal. But I got the nine millimeter out anyway, and took the creaky wooden stairs as quietly as I could manage — shit, probably took me two or three minutes to get to the top. All the way up I was wondering what I'd do if that door was locked. Forcing it would be no problem, but it might leave a visual record of my entry, plus if anybody was up there, I'd be announcing myself more obnoxiously than I cared to. . . .

But it wasn't locked.

I eased the thing open, and it didn't make any more noise than the Crypt Keeper's vault, though it didn't matter a damn. Nobody was in the kitchen, which was where I came out. Nothing was in the kitchen, except a dead refrigerator that dated back to Betty Furness days, no kitchen table, nothing except a counter and sink and empty cupboards.

We'll skip the suspense stuff — nobody was in the house. I searched it slow and careful, because that's what you do in such a case; but the place had not a stick of furniture in it, much less a person. Even the flotsam and jetsam of the lives lived here by good solid immigrant stock for maybe a hundred years had gone to Dumpster heaven.

I should have said "no stick of furniture" *original* to the house, because in the living room, by the front bay-type window, was some recently-brought-in stuff that indicated the presence of a human being, not a rodent (except maybe figuratively).

The blond kid's set-up included a folding chair, the beach variety (Mike Love again), like he'd been sitting by a pool or maybe on the deck of cruise ship, and not in the front room of an old farmhouse where he could maintain surveillance on the target of a contract killing. He had a portable radio with cassette player that ran off batteries (yes, Poison tapes), and a Styrofoam chest with ice keeping cans of Pepsi cold as well as a few wrapped Casey's General Store sandwiches. Some small packets of potato chips leaned against the Styrofoam chest, and a pair of binoculars rested on the window ledge. Having searched the house, I'd already determined that the toilets still worked, so he had a decent stakeout post here, though my own back couldn't have stood that flimsy chair for days on end.

If the fact that he was a Pepsi drinker wasn't disgusting enough, I noted to one side of the beach chair a pile of *Hustler* magazines, a box of Kleenex, some baby oil, and a metal wastebasket filled with crumpled, wadded tissues, which told me more about how the blond kid dealt with boredom than I wanted to know.

For two hours and maybe fifteen minutes, I sat in his beach chair, long enough to get so thirsty I almost drank one of his damn Pepsis. I used the binoculars and could see the Paddlewheel okay, but without any meaningful view into a window. The late afternoon turned blue and then black. The house was warm and stuffy at first and then, without the sun, got cool and stuffy. At one point, I thumbed through a *Hustler,* but did not partake of the baby oil and Kleenex. I was raised on *Playboy* and still preferred Hefner's fantasy to Flynt's gynecology.

The kid drove a Mustang (I'd seen it parked next to Monahan's Buick at the Wheelhouse Motel) whose headlights announced him when he pulled into the mouth of the drive. What followed was a graceless dance: he got out and unlocked and moved the metal gate, returned to the car, pulled in deeper, got out and locked up again, then back in his car to come crunching up the gravel drive.

When he unlocked the kitchen door and came in, I was to one side and put the nose of the nine millimeter in his neck. By now it was dark in the house, but some moonlight filtered in the dirty cracked windows over the filthy old sink and I could see his blue eyes pop. They were light blue and looked spooky in the dimness. I mean the room's dimness, not his.

"Hands on your head," I said.

He put them there. The eyes stayed wide. He was even skinnier, close up — still in the black *Poison* t-shirt, but a light tan jacket open over it. He had a snubby .38 in a jacket pocket. I took it, slipped it in my left-hand windbreaker pocket.

"Let's talk," I said.

He said, in a husky tenor, "Who the fuck are you?"

"Not cops."

He swallowed. "Then *what* are you?"

"An interloper."

"What the fuck's an interloper?"

"A guy who noticed what you're up to, and wants in."

He frowned. Thinking took effort; it even made lines in his boyish face. By the way, I made him for maybe twenty-five.

He asked, "What do you mean, 'wants in'?"

"Sit down."

"Where? Do you see a fuckin' chair?"

"I see the fuckin' floor."

"It's filthy."

"I don't think I mind."

He sat, cross-legged, Indian-style. He folded his arms, as if that would protect him. He looked up at me, like an inexperienced girl afraid of her first blow job.

I said, "Who's the target?"

"What do you mean?"

"This is going to go very slow if you keep asking me that."

"Well, I don't know what the fuck you mean."

I slapped him with the nine millimeter. Not hard enough to cut the flesh, just to get his attention, and to give me time to take the noise suppressor from my right-hand windbreaker pocket and affix it to the nine millimeter's snout.

Seeing the silencer bothered him more than the love pat.

"I don't dig roughing guys up," I told him, meaning it. "But I can shoot a kneecap off and live with it. Assuming you don't pass out, you'll get talkative. You won't annoy me with dumb questions."

"It's a guy named Cornell. Richard Cornell."

"What does he do?"

I thought, *Runs the Paddlewheel.*

"He runs that club across the way — the Paddlewheel."

"Who hired you?"

"Doesn't work that way."

"You work through a middleman?"

He swallowed again and nodded. "Are you one of us or something?"

"How's it going down?"

"Parking lot."

"After closing?"

He nodded.

"How late does the Paddlewheel stay open?"

"Late. Five A.M. That's the point."

"The point?"

"The point of Haydee's Port. The point of the Paddlewheel. Across the river, they have to close at one A.M. People drive over to keep partying."

"Is it dawn by five A.M.?"

"Why don't you get a fucking almanac? Jesus."

I shot him twice, *thup thup,* once for each eye of the skull on his Poison t-shirt. It was a smart-ass thing to do, but then I was responding to a smart-ass remark. The blood that spattered on the old fridge behind him gave the old kitchen a dash of color, even in the near dark.

It could use it.

The pain in the ass part came next, and I'll spare you most of it. I had to get the keys for that gate out of his jacket pocket, then had to walk down through the cornfield to my car and bring it around and go through the gate routine myself and then back the Sunbird up to the rear steps.

Finally I dragged the kid across the ancient linoleum — he made a snail's trail of blood slime — and down the steps, his head bumping and clunking down, and pretty soon I had him up and in the trunk.

An argument could be made for leaving him there on the dirty kitchen floor, but I felt I wanted his body in the trunk, in case later on I needed to make a point.

It got your attention, didn't it?

Two

The sky was full of stars with a nearly full moon that gave the outdoors a nice ivory tinge. I was floating on my back in the Wheelhouse Motel pool, feeling pretty mellow for a guy who had just killed somebody. A guy who before long would probably be killing somebody else.

I could even see my Sunbird from here, parked at Unit 28 on the same wing of the motel where Monahan's Buick still occupied Unit 36's slot. The adjacent slot yawned empty. I figured the blond kid had checked out before he went over to take his farmhouse stakeout one last time; with the job set for dawn, he would have had no reason to go back to the motel.

And yet he *had* come back in a way, because right now he was in the trunk of that Sunbird. But who could argue that — one way or another (to quote Debbie Harry) — he hadn't already checked out?

In my mellow, floating state, I wondered if I was getting over-confident, even cocky. I had checked into the same goddamn motel as Monahan . . . with his dead partner in my trunk. Of course, my other choices would have been to stay across the river in River Bluff at a Holiday Inn or some shit, or risk the sperm-infused sheets of the Eezer Inn (and I was way too squeamish for that).

Even my only precaution — wrapping my nine millimeter in a towel, stowed poolside under a deck-style chair — was risky. What if somebody kicked or otherwise moved the bundle, and the damn automatic clunked out on the concrete? Went off, even?

You might even say it looked a little suspicious, because I'd draped another towel on the chair itself. . . .

On the other hand, there were no other swimmers in the early evening at the Paddlewheel's pool. An hour ago, I'd had a piece of pie (butterscotch cream) at the restaurant and an older gal named Marge had chatted with me, starting with answering my query about why the restaurant was so dead at supper time.

"The Paddlewheel opens at five," she said.

"Also closes at five, I understand."

She nodded. Brunette, brown-eyed, she

was pushing fifty and just a little heavy, with a lined face and neck that weren't enough to conceal how attractive she'd once been.

"We're just a kind of annex over here," she said. "We run an hourly shuttle over there and everything."

"To the Paddlewheel? Really."

"Really. Anybody staying with us is here for the Paddlewheel, and they almost all take supper over there. We make it on breakfast and lunch and really do pretty well right up to late afternoon."

"How long has the Paddlewheel been around?"

"Going on ten years. It's on its third management, British 'bloke' named Cornell, Richard Cornell — but everybody calls him Dickie. Real smoothie. He's the boss here. He built the Wheelhouse, and he's done wonders with the Paddlewheel. Oh, it was *always* nice, you know, always the respectable entertainment alternative in Haydee's. But Dickie upgraded everything — food, entertainment, even expanded the gambling."

"How can you be respectable running an illegal casino?"

She shrugged, refilling my iced tea from a pitcher. "Haydee's has always been a wide-open little town. It's like Reno or Vegas."

"This isn't Nevada."

"No, honey, it's Illinois." She grinned like a female wolf; her bridgework could have been better. "And last I looked, Chicago was in Illinois, too, right?"

She had a point.

So I had the pool to myself. That I was feeling this mellow was either a testament to my self-confidence or my self-delusion. Still, it was nice knowing I could have that much caffeine (I'd consumed more than my share of Diet Coke and iced tea today) and still feel this laid-back.

Plus (as I say) I'd killed a guy, who was currently in my trunk in my line of vision, and it didn't seem to faze me, though the ass of the buggy was thumbing its nose at me. Idly I hoped that trunk didn't leak. Be a bitch if it were seeping red stuff the way the late blond kid's Mustang had dripped oil.

I wanted to make sure I was relaxed before I went over to the Paddlewheel. No reason to go in right at five P.M. — last thing I needed, either for my own peace of mind or for staying inconspicuous, was to be a new patron who dropped in and stayed for twelve hours. I figured going over around nine should do it. Time would be required to make contact with Richard Cornell, but that should be plenty. And I could grab a late bite.

My mellowness took a hit, however, when a memory floated into the stream of my consciousness like a turd in the pool.

I had heard of Haydee's Port before. And I'd heard of the Paddlewheel, too. . . .

About eight years ago, the very first time I utilized the Broker's list, I'd helped out a guy who ran a much smaller casino in the hinterlands near Des Moines. His name was Frank Tree, and he'd filled me in on his personal history, and part of it had been running the Paddlewheel in Haydee's Port. He'd sold the place, and that was all I knew about it.

This had just been a stray piece of information that hadn't been pertinent to the job at hand — which had been keeping Tree from getting killed — and it was a small miracle that this trivia occurred to me now.

I doubted this information had any current pertinence, either; but it troubled me that the synapses in my brain hadn't sparked immediately. Christ, I was only in my mid-thirties. How could my memory let me down like that?

Physically, I felt up to whatever came along. I was no muscleman, but swam often, usually daily — it was the variety of physical exercise I preferred, and helped me relax, and allowed my thoughts to either fade or come into focus, as the case might be. Out here, on my back, staring at the stars and moon over Haydee's Port, clarity was the result.

Maybe it was time to retire the Broker's list. Maybe I was getting too casual about killing, or cocky or sloppy or whatever. After all, I had an investment opportunity back in Wisconsin, where I lived, and if I could make enough of a killing on this job — again, of the financial variety — it could be the last one.

Maybe a hired assassin has a natural working life, like an athlete or a rock star or a sex symbol. . . .

For some time, I'd lived in an A-frame cottage on small, private Paradise Lake, which suffered few of the tourists that haunted the nearby Lake Geneva vacation center. The scattering of summer homes meant I had very few neighbors off-season, which was how I liked it, and even on-season was no problem.

One business did serve the year-round locals, and in summer attracted a small, tolerable number of tourists: Wilma's Welcome Inn, a rambling two-story structure that had been a roadhouse back in Prohibition Days, converted in the only slightly-less-distant past to a restaurant, gas station, and hotel (a convenience store was a more recent touch, taking the place of a gift shop). Everything was under one rustic, slightly ramshackle roof.

Wilma had been a beautiful woman trapped in a tub of lard, and one of the few humans I ever really liked, in part because she made a great bowl of chili and also because she was pleasantly chatty without getting nosy. She was dead now, and her boyfriend/bartender Charley was trying to run the place, doing a fairly crap job of it. Her daughter was a curvy little babe in her late teens who wanted to sell the place before Charley ran it into the lake, so she could move to California and do drugs.

I apologize for all this extraneous shit, but the bottom line is, I had a chance to buy the place. As a kid back in Ohio, I'd tinkered with cars and worked in a garage, so the gas station part appealed to me. I'd be handy enough to whip the dump into shape with remedial repairs, plus I'd made the acquaintance of a woman in Lake Geneva who knew restaurants and hotels and was looking for a new position. The first new position I tried involved her getting fucked against a door, and screaming like she'd just won the lottery, so I thought she might make a reasonably interesting employee.

Maybe this was that crossroads moment you hear so much about. Maybe if I survived this job, and came out of it with a nice payday, I could go straight. After all, a lot about what I did had drawbacks — long travel hours, the endless surveillance, occasional shitty accommodations, inconsistent food. Sometimes the nine millimeter could jam.

I swam laps, once back and forth quickly, then just settled in at an easy lope. The pool was cool but not cold, heated but not too. If it's like a bath, I get sleepy, and I never like to be *that* relaxed, unless I'm in my own home with the alarm system on. Back home, I swam in the lake, when weather allowed, and at the Lake Geneva YMCA, where I had a membership, staying clear of the steam room. On the road, the motel/hotel pools seemed evenly divided between indoor and outdoor. But on a warm night like this, with the water just a little crisp, nothing could beat the Great Out Of Doors.

I did some lazy laps on my back, so I could watch the stars and moon. For some reason, I thought about the Broker. Maybe it was because of the pool at the Concort Inn, a hotel in the Quad Cities the Broker worked out of, and while that pool was indoors, it had a skylight. Swimming indoors under the stars creates a dreamy sensation. Memorable one, too. I'd swum there a number of times, and again my memory was making odd connections.

When the Broker approached me, I'd been living in a fleabag hotel in Los Angeles. Drinking is not generally my thing, but it had been then. Still Coke, only with Bacardi. *Lots* of Bacardi — one Coke can to a bottle of rum, yo ho ho.

He was a handsome white-haired, white-mustached businessman who wore tailored suits and spoke in speeches, and he might have been forty or he might have been sixty — I never asked or bothered to find out. He thought I might be interested in doing for good money (for him) what I had previously done in Vietnam for shit change (for Uncle Sam) — namely, killing people.

I'd been good at it. I'd been a sniper most of the time in Nam, though I did make it through my share of firefights, and I probably caused a couple dozen yellow melons to splatter and send their bearers into whatever their idea of the afterlife was. In sniper work particularly, you find yourself picking off people like a game of *Galaga,* but with better effects.

None of that got me in trouble. In fact, it got me some medals. What got me in trouble was coming home, finding my wife in bed with a guy and killing the son of a bitch. Actually, that's wrong — I didn't kill him till the next day when I went over to the prick's house to have it out with him, and he was under his car working on it, and said, "What the fuck do you want *now,* bunghole?"

And I kicked the jack out.

This made it look premeditated (if it had been premeditated, I'd have taken a gun) and made it harder for the unwritten law to kick in. But the papers took my side and I ended up not getting prosecuted, at which point the papers did *not* take my side. This is the only time I got any publicity for anybody I ever killed, incidentally, and it's apparently what inspired the Broker to look me up.

I haven't given you my name, and won't, but Broker knew it all right (it was in his file), though he immediately gave me a one-name alias — Quarry — which he insisted on using. He had these kind of corny code names for all of us — Monahan was "Driver" in the file, I would later learn.

Anyway, I got comfortable with "Quarry," and other people in the business called me that, too. Sometimes I even used it on the job with a first name stuck on. Right now, though, at the Wheelhouse, I was checked in as Jack Gibson.

I sensed someone had joined me, not in the pool but taking a deck chair alongside, and I stopped swimming except to stroke over and climb out and sit on the edge, water dripping off, catching my breath.

Across the pool, in the chair next to the one that had my towel draped over it (and my towel-wrapped gun under it), Monahan was sitting. Beyond him, just over his right shoulder, I could see the Sunbird.

"Lovely night," I said.

He was smoking. On his left was a little glass table with his Chesterfields and room key on it and a folded towel. He was in a pair of navy swim trunks and a red t-shirt. His legs and arms were hairless, and he looked much younger than his forty or so years. He had dark eyes and pale skin and looked relaxed, head back, blowing smoke rings for his own amusement. He had the kind of nasty, smirky face that fraternity boys never grow out of.

"A little humid," he said.

His voice echoed across the water.

"Could rain," I admitted, mine echoing similarly. "But you can't bitch about the temperature."

"Sure I can." He lowered his chin and grinned at me.

Was it just a dumb remark, or was there something in it?

I stretched, then walked around the pool — diving board was at the other end — and knelt to retrieve the two towels under my chair. One, of course, was rolled up like an ice cream cake with a nine millimeter center. I sat down, placed the bundle as inconspicuously as possible on the cement to my right — Monahan was seated at my left — and began toweling off casually.

"Looks like all the sweet pussy took a walk," he said with a sneer.

I wasn't sure I got that, but figuring he meant the bikini girls, I tried this: "Lotta nice stuff gettin' strutted this afternoon, all right. I guess they're all over at the Paddlewheel."

He nodded. Smoked some more. No more rings. "This motel's the loneliest place in town, after dark."

"Rough little burg," I noted.

"Paddlewheel's safe enough. Games are straight. Good food. Decent entertainment." He shook his head. Blew dragon smoke out his nostrils. "But you can get your ass handed to you downtown, brother."

46

"Yeah?"

"Joint called the Lucky Devil, especially."

"Rough?"

"Rougher than a cob." He extended a hand. "Sam Mason. Insurance game."

I shook it. "Jack Gibson. Veterinary medicine."

"Really? Pets or farm animals?"

"Know much about farms?"

"Was raised on one."

I gave him half a grin. "Me? Wouldn't know a heifer from a hog. My line of meds is strictly the pet trade."

He laughed and smoke came out. "You want to make a buck in this hellhole? Try selling penicillin."

"Not at the Paddlewheel, though. . . ."

"No! No. I don't even think any high-class ass works out of there. Bluff City is too smalltown for call girls, and the kind of girls you meet on the Haydee's side, you don't take home to mother . . . unless mother is a doctor specializing in the clap."

I shook my head, did a little shiver. "Since AIDS came around, Mrs. Gibson's little boy don't go out in the rain without his rubbers."

"Ha! Don't blame you. I'm a happily married man with a beautiful wife. Two healthy kids. I wouldn't risk all that, fooling around

47

with some trashy little cunt."

I grinned at him, recalling the carry-out cutie back home. "What about the little beauties who were sunning themselves this afternoon?"

"I'm married," he said with a grin, "not dead."

Yet.

"I still have a pulse myself," I said.

"You're not tied down?"

"Nope." I nodded toward the memory of the bikini girls around the pool. "What do you think, they're college girls?"

"The ones today? They're secretaries and office workers from St. Louis, on holiday."

"You talk to 'em?"

"Maybe a little." He grinned again. "No charge for looking. But there are some college girls from Iowa City checked in, too. This is nice, young, sweet pussy, my friend. Looking to be naughty. It'd be a sin not to help 'em out. Downright fucking unkind."

Not only had he already forgotten the beautiful wife, the Chinese chickie was yesterday's carry-out, too.

"Well," I said, and reached down for the rolled towel, then slipped my hand inside, around the nine millimeter's grip, "nice meeting you."

The silencer wasn't attached, but the

towel would muffle a shot, though the cloth would likely catch fire.

He grinned again. "Don't do anything I wouldn't do," he said.

"I think I can keep that promise," I said.

I didn't see where he could have a gun on him, not in swim trunks and t-shirt, but I took no chances, walking at an angle to my room, keeping the seated man in my eyeline.

As I reached my door, I saw him get up and slip off the shirt, his body ghostly pale in the moonlight. He dove in. He was doing his own laps as I went inside.

The bed cut the room nearly in half, and I sat on its edge facing the door with the gun in my hand, trained there. I was still in my trunks, which were damp, and I wasn't completely dry myself. Then it occurred to me that if he was brazen enough to shoot through the door, he might get me.

So I moved down the bed, near the headboard, and sat and waited.

Nothing.

That had just been talk, right? Friendly talk? Guy stuff? He was staying here, I was staying here, two fellas taking a swim and striking up a conversation. He had a job to do but wouldn't necessarily head over to the Paddlewheel till near dawn, when the time came to execute his plan. It was not at all unnatural for him to relax by the pool, to swim, to chat amiably with another guest. He had time to kill.

Could he have discovered his partner was dead?

I had the body, of course, but I hadn't cleaned up after myself except to remove fingerprints. Blood was still on the refrigerator, and on the floor, and even on the back steps and driveway gravel — crusty and dark by now, but unmistakably blood, especially to a pro like Monahan. A clean kill in that the guy went quickly, but otherwise sloppy.

Like me?

Was I too sloppy and stupid to survive?

I showered and sat up on the bed in my shorts with a gun in my hand watching an old movie on Turner Classics. Monahan did not come knocking, and for that matter did not come *not* knocking. . . .

This was what I got for staying at the same goddamn motel as my target. Perhaps I should just get in the Sunbird, dump the blond kid's body along the road somewhere, and head back to Wisconsin. This was feeling like too much risk, with too much exposure. Sure, I had invested some time and money and spent a couple of nine millimeter slugs on Mike Love. But why chance it?

On the other hand, I was still about twenty grand short of what I needed to buy Wilma's Welcome Inn. I wasn't in a position to get a bank loan. I needed cash.

So I put on my Don Johnson duds and headed over to the Paddlewheel.

THREE

I pulled in about nine-thirty and found the big parking lot nearly full, the Paddlewheel doing remarkable business for a Wednesday night. At the far end, a brown-and-gold vehicle emblazoned SHERIFF'S DEPARTMENT was parked by a fence, nose forward, with what I presumed was an off-duty deputy sitting there to provide security. His windows were down and he was smoking — the amber eye of his cigarette and his vague shape were all I could make out.

His presence didn't alarm me — I'd have been surprised if some off-duty law enforcement rep *hadn't* been so employed here — but neither did it mean the master of the Paddlewheel castle was safe from becoming the victim of a hit-and-run in his own parking lot. Only after its closing around dawn, with the target leaving the building to head for his own parked car in an otherwise empty lot, security deputy long gone, would

Monahan practice his vehicular artistry.

I backed my Sunbird into a space in a row parallel to the river, leaving a little room to get around to the trunk, where the blond kid was sound asleep, the little angel. After folding it inside a road map, I tucked the nine millimeter in the glove compartment, having no intention of walking into the place armed. Holsters, shoulder or belt, weren't my style, and I couldn't risk that kind of lump under the lightweight white jacket.

Having parked fairly close, I felt loose and at ease — I'd willed myself to leave any misgivings behind, and anyway, the warm night and the cool breeze were battling in a gentle, soothing way. Nothing about Monahan's poolside behavior gave me reason to believe he'd made me — actually, quite the opposite.

Still, he was a pro and not to be underestimated; he could easily have been playing me. And because this was a speculative project, I had the ability to bail at any time. True, I'd spent some money and had strained my lower back a little, stuffing that blond punk in the trunk. But I still could say fuck it and go home to my A-frame on the lake.

Nice to have options.

The big old brick building that housed the Paddlewheel had been built into the small rise along the river so that its lower level was underground except on the Mississippi side (back when the structure had been a warehouse, that was where goods could be on- and off-loaded). That meant you entered from the parking lot onto the second floor.

I moved past a coat check area and restrooms to a hostess station, where a good-looking brunette in a white tuxedo blouse and long black skirt with high-heel boots was currently occupied with a quartet of couples who hadn't bothered with a reservation. So I didn't have to deal with her right away, and could get the lay of the land.

Down a few steps from this entryway was a long dining room, with tables covered in white cloth with glowing red candles, and a big mural of a paddlewheel boat along the left wall, a magnificent picture-window river view at the far end. There were a few empty tables but, for this time of night mid-week in the Midwest, the dining room was bustling.

A bar was at right, and it was crowded, too, possibly with diners waiting for a table. The smoky area had red-covered booths against a wall newer than the other sandblasted brick ones, indicating the floor had been halved to allow for kitchen and possibly offices. Tucked in the corner was a small stage with a pianist in a tux at a baby grand, noodling show tunes; a stool at a mike indicated a singer was part of the mix, but not right now.

The help's attire was on the formal side — waitresses in white tuxedo blouses and black trousers — while the patrons ran the gamut: guys in everything from leather jackets and stonewashed jeans to suits and ties (though my Armani over a Ralph Lauren tee was about par) and the women sporting designer shit including plenty of shoulder pads and big earrings and miniskirts and feathered hair. But everybody seemed to be spruced up, at least their idea of it.

The group at the hostess station was getting irritable — they could see enough open seating to service them — and the brunette was patiently explaining that it would take a while to put some tables together, and if they'd just go to the bar, she'd call them.

I had no problem. I even got a table by the picture window, and all it had cost me was my charming smile. The river was reflecting the moon and a silver-ivory shimmer made it very romantic, except for the part where I was sitting at a table for two by myself.

The food wasn't pricey — my assumption was, the casino was the money maker — and I took my time eating a fried scallops dinner, including their "signature" beer-battered baked potato. The thing was pretty good, even if it didn't rise to the status of a Famous Bacon Cheeseburger.

This far down from the bar, the piano noodling was fairly distant, and didn't cover up the low-end pounding of drums and bass guitar above. Couldn't pick any tunes out, but you could tell it was rock and not country. Between whatever songs were going on up there, you could make out the muffled music of slots and poker machines below, playing their bells-and-whistles refrain.

I killed maybe an hour with the meal, which included two glasses of Diet Coke with twists of lime. I left the waitress a nice tip, then walked back to the restrooms, to get rid of some of the cola. I noticed an elevator tucked back behind the coat check, and went over to the hostess to ask her about it.

"Is that for the casino?" I asked her.

She had big brown eyes and lots of blue eye shadow that clashed, but her lips were full and red-lipsticked, so I forgave her.

Friendly but guarded, she said, "That's for our Key Club."

"Ah. How do you join?"

"You take that elevator down, and go to the window that says 'New Members.' "

"Cool. Thanks."

So I had a look at the casino. First I joined, of course, and it cost all of ten bucks. I wasn't sure how joining made this any more legal, but it must have had something to do with the arrangement with the local law. The "New Members" window was just one of half a dozen cages, the rest of which were to buy or cash in chips.

The casino wasn't the Flamingo but, for the middle of the Midwest, was impressive enough. Certainly was hopping, a couple hundred guests partaking of half a dozen blackjack tables, a trio of roulette wheels, the latest Vegas-style slots on one side, video poker on the other. The far end had a bar with some booth seating along another river-view window.

What decoration there was ran to riverboat stuff, paintings of Bret Maverick-type gamblers and Mark Twain in a captain's hat and paddlewheels on the river. Mostly, though, the room was just a charmless space of sandblasted brick walls crammed with

gambling gear. I noted a security staff —
rugged-looking characters in black trousers
and red satin vests and white shirts with
string ties and no name tags, all blessed with
the craggy, humorless mien of the strip-club
bouncer.

I counted six of these characters, roam-
ing, keeping a hard eye on things, occasionally communicating with either a boss or
their musclebound brethren by walkie-
talkie.

I had a beer in the casino bar, served by a
perky little redheaded waitress in a red satin
outfit that was little more than a low-cut
one-piece bathing suit with mesh stockings
and black heels; if her push-up bra had
pushed any harder, her nipples would've
popped out.

Half a dozen little booby-displaying beauties were weaving around the casino, providing free drinks. I made conversation with
mine and learned she was a community college student across the river — most of the
girls were.

"So," I asked her, "you don't live in Haydee's Port?"

"No!" she said, eyes so wide you'd think I
goosed her. "*Nobody* lives in Haydee's Port!"

"What about your boss?"

She got coy. "What boss is that?"

"Mr. Cornell. Does he live across the river, too?"

My knowing the boss's name was enough for her to replace coy with chatty. "He lives close. A regular mansion. Ever see *Gone with the Wind*?"

"Sure."

"Like that. White pillars and everything."

"He lives in Tara and you're a wage slave, huh?"

"Yeah, minimum wage, but the tips are good."

I considered kidding her about darkies all working on the Mississippi, but figured the reference would be lost on her.

"Kind of business this place does," I said, "I'm not surprised Mr. Cornell has a mansion. He here tonight?"

"He's always here. I've been at the Paddlewheel a year, and he's never missed a night."

"Could you point him out to me?"

She shook her head. "He's rarely in the Key Club, unless he's in the back poker room."

"Is he in the back poker room now?"

"No." She got narrow-eyed. "Why?"

"Just like to meet him. Tell him how impressed I am. I mean, I'd heard about this place, but it exceeds all my expectations."

She liked that. Apparently she was a proud little community-college student/waitress. "Yes! I don't know of anything like it anywhere else around these parts."

These parts? My God, this *was* the Midwest. . . .

I asked, "What about downtown?"

The eyes got the goosed look again. "In Haydee's Port? You don't want to go down there, sir."

"I don't?"

"No! It's just for lowlifes."

So I left her a nice tip. She didn't consider me a lowlife, and that made me feel good about myself.

I gambled a little. Lost twenty-five bucks at blackjack, got ahead fifty at roulette. Played video poker, a buck a shot, and in ninety minutes carved the fifty in half. Another waitress, who I'd asked for a Diet Coke, delivered it.

I asked her, "The music upstairs?"

She had a galaxy of permed blonde hair and dark blue eyes and light blue eyeshadow and big breasts that made heavy lifting for the push-up bra. "You mean upstairs at the Paddlewheel Lounge?"

"I'm talking about the top floor."

"So am I."

"How long does the music last?"

60

"Till two on weeknights. All night Friday and Saturday. We're closed Sunday."

Even Hades rested on the seventh day, it seemed, this branch office, anyway.

It was already close to one A.M., so I took the elevator up to the Paddlewheel Lounge. The big room had lots of neon pseudo-graffiti on the brick walls, glowing in black light — cheesy stuff that tried too hard, jagged lettering of assorted words and phrases: *Da Bomb!, Awesome!, Wicked!, Rad!, Gnarly!*

Not that the crowd seemed to mind, a mix of twenty-and thirty-somethings, some of whom I'd seen dining downstairs. The dance floor was a raised acrylic platform with red-yellow-blue flashing lights inside, the band fronting big amplifiers on a wooden platform stage (the drummer up on his own smaller one) painted flat black but with more corny neon day-glo fake graffiti. The little dance platform could only accommodate maybe a third of the hundred or so in the lounge, so a lot of smoking and talking (that is, shouting over the band) was going on at the little round tables with red vinyl cloths.

A bar was at one end, as far away from the band as possible. The bartender was female, a pretty blonde with over-teased hair and a black leather vest over her white blouse; she wasn't particularly busty, which was almost a relief after all those exploding bosoms in the casino.

Perched on a stool, I ordered another Diet Coke and asked her (actually, yelled at her), *"What's it like on the weekends?"*

"Zoo-a-rama," she shouted back with a friendly smile and an eyeball roll. *"Hangin' off the flippin' rafters, my friend."*

"Good band!"

They were — they were doing "Under My Thumb" by the Stones. They all wore white shirts and skinny black ties and black leather trousers and short spiky hair, including the lead singer, a cute skinny girl.

"Not bad," she admitted. *"Smart. Called the Nodes. They play about half classic rock and half New Wave. That's why the demo is so broad."*

"The demo?"

"Demographic. You'll find 'em as young as twenty-one and as old as forty, out there."

Forty didn't sound as old to me as it used to. Also, I thought some of the girls — like one in a side ponytail, fingerless gloves and a petticoat, who was just swishing by — weren't twenty-one. Not that I could imagine the Paddlewheel was a rigorous I.D. checker.

That was all the shouted speech I could take, so I got out the charming smile again and made sure the teased-hairdo behind the bar got a nice tip, figuring she was another minimum-wage slave.

I'd been on all three floors of the Paddle-wheel now, over these past three hours or so, and still hadn't seen Richard Cornell, at least not to my knowledge. I really didn't have any idea what he looked like, just that he was a Brit and a "smoothie." All I probably needed to do was ask somebody who appeared to be vaguely in management if I could see Mr. Cornell. But I wasn't ready to stoop that low just yet. . . .

On the second floor, things were winding down. The dining room had closed at midnight, though the bar was still heavily populated, serving booze and sandwiches till 4 A.M., if the menu was to be believed. I was seated at a little table whose round top was smaller than a steering wheel, having another Diet Coke, listening to the vocalist who had finally turned up on stage to keep the pianist company.

A couple of things had become clear about Richard Cornell's management style, among them that he paid minimum wage, but chiefly that if you weren't a good-looking young woman, you need not apply for any job that included interacting with the public. The needle on the pulchritude meter at this place was buried, or wanted to be. Till it closed in '81, the Playboy Club at Lake Geneva had been my favorite home away from home, and the Paddlewheel rivaled their Bunnies with these cornfed cuties.

But the woman on the small stage, perched on a stool, was not cute, nor was she young. I made her for mid-forties, easy. She was a little heavy and she had some years on her, but she blew the cuties away, because she was beautiful. Truly beautiful.

She had reddish blond widow's-peaked hair that was up off her high forehead but swept down to her bare shoulders. Her wide-set eyes were green and so was her eyeshadow, her face a gentle oval nicely disrupted by prominent cheekbones; her lips were full and ripe and glistening red. She wore a bare-shouldered black dress with a full skirt, the top part putting half of an admirable full bosom on display, no push-up bra, though some would argue she could use one — I would argue she'd never lack for a man to push them up for her.

When I sat down, she was singing "What Is This Thing Called Love?" She had a soft, smoky voice that reminded me of Julie

London — she reminded me physically of Julie London, too, though the nose was different, small, almost pug. Everything she did was sad but with a lilting, mid-tempo swing feel that was part her and part the deft piano player.

Some people were talking, laughing, at their tables, because for anybody not gambling, it was getting pretty drunk out. But perhaps half of the little crowd of maybe twenty-five at the tiny tables in front of the small stage were paying rapt attention.

I had a feeling she had a following. She might have made it big in another era — she was old enough that she might have tried, before she'd become a throwback, if a goddamn pure one. Anybody else would have been using a drum machine and a synthesizer. Yet somehow she was getting away with just her voice and a piano, right here in the middle of the USA, closer to the Gran' Ole Opry in Nashville than the Rainbow Room in Manhattan.

She sang "Little White Lies" with a lot of humor and warmth, and then she slowed down "I Got Lost in His Arms" with such a rich, well-earned vibrato that I damn near remembered how to cry.

Rising, she got a nice hand as she smiled and nodded, gestured to her pianist, who was bald and bespectacled and maybe thirty and painfully skinny; then they both got some more applause and came down off the stage.

On impulse, I rose and went over to her. "Excuse me," I said. "But that was terrific."

She seemed embarrassed. "Oh. Well. Thank you. Haven't seen you here before."

"Passing through."

She grinned and it was wide and real with plenty of white. "Nobody passes through Haydee's Port."

"Passing through River Bluff. Can I buy you a drink?"

The smile tightened, the teeth disappearing. "No. I have one more set in fifteen minutes. I never take a drink till after my last set. But you're very kind."

"Coffee, then."

"Makes me jumpy."

"Perrier? Not coming on to you. Just liked what I heard."

The teeth returned. "Nice young man like you, maybe I wouldn't mind."

"A Perrier?"

"You coming on to me." The smile tightened again but in a nice way, this time. "Come on."

She took me by the arm and led me to a booth with a RESERVED card on it. I sat opposite her as she retrieved a purse from somewhere. This booth was apparently her between-sets office. She got out Paddle-wheel matches and a pack of Virginia Slims.

She offered me a smoke and I declined. When a waitress came over, my new friend indeed ordered a Perrier and I had the same. She got a cig going, waved the match out and gave me a skeptical look.

"You aren't gay, are you?"

"No. Why?"

"You're about . . . Beatles age, I'd say. Rolling Stones. Your idea of a female singer would be, what? Petula Clark? Dusty Springfield?"

"What's wrong with them?"

"Nothing. But most guys your age who think Cole Porter and Rodgers and Hart are the shit are gay." She nodded toward where her piano player sat with another young guy at a table. "Lonnie's gay, as you might have guessed. Where would I find a straight kid who could play like that?"

I skipped any comment on Lonnie, and went to her first point. "Maybe I just have a healthy respect for professionalism."

She seemed to like that.

I sipped my sparkling water and hauled out the charming smile again, which was getting a workout tonight. "My next line is,

'What's a nice girl like you doing in a place like this?' "

She blew a smoky kiss at me. "I'm part owner of it. I can do what I like."

"Part owner? I, uh . . . I came in on your act. I didn't catch your name. Mine's Jack, by the way. Jack Gibson."

"Two of my favorite things — money and a mixed drink." Her laugh was husky as she extended a hand for me to take and shake. "I'm Angela Dell."

"I thought this place was owned by a guy named Cornell."

"Dickie is my husband. Dell is my stage name — a shortened version of my maiden name. I used it before I met Dickie, and I've kept it."

"You've been doing this a while."

"Singing? Oh yes."

"Do any recording?"

She nodded, twitched a smile that was more for her than me. "Had a contract with Verve back in the '60s."

"No kidding?"

That was a big deal — Verve was a jazz label and very picky about the artists they signed.

I went on: "I'm surprised I haven't heard any of your records."

"They just put one album out, and it sank

like a stone."

"I'd love to hear it."

She shrugged. "You can buy it at the bar — I got the rights back to put it out on CD and cassette. There are two newer ones, too, recorded with just Lonnie on the piano."

"You'll sign them?"

"Sure." She tapped her cigarette into a glass tray with a Paddlewheel logo in its bottom. "What do you do, Jack?"

"Nothing very interesting, I'm afraid. I sell veterinary medicine."

"Really? What kind?"

"Do you know anything about farms?"

"No. I have a cat, though."

"Well, I strictly sell to vets who service farms. Pretty boring."

"But you're on the road a lot?"

"Yes. You must've been, too, at one time."

She nodded. "Until I married Dickie."

I was trying to figure out a way to finesse this, to use my new acquaintance with the missus to get to the man of the house, or anyway of the Paddlewheel.

Then she said, "But don't let that discourage you."

There was something sly in the green eyes now, and the full mouth was twisted up at one corner.

"Pardon?" I managed.

"Dickie and I are separated. We . . . we'd probably have been divorced a long time ago, but I'm a Catholic, and I don't want to go to hell . . . even if I *do* work in Haydee's."

"Oh-kay," I said.

"We're friendly, Dickie and I. Best of buddies. He's got a great business head, and I add a little class to the joint. I don't have any desire to do anything in life but sing for my supper. No ambition — not for a new man, or an old career. Anyway, a shopworn broad like me can't make it in show biz these days, that's for sure."

"I'd think some lounge in Vegas would —"

"I worked a lounge in Vegas for six years. It wasn't a bad life, but it was a dead end, and here I'm a co-owner and making nice money and singing six nights a week. Satisfies my work ethic and my artistic cravings, and fills my bank account. I live in a nice apartment over in River Bluff, just me and my pussy . . . cat."

That pause was promising.

"How long," she asked, tapping her ash off in the tray, "are you going to be in town?"

"Not sure. Few days. Maybe we could get together. Have lunch or something."

She shrugged. "I only have another half hour set. Why don't you stick around? We

70

could go over to the Wheelhouse and have breakfast. They're open twenty-four hours."

Then she smiled, sighed smoke dreamily, stubbed out her cigarette, and headed up onto the stage, swaying her hips a little, whether for the audience or me, I couldn't say. But she had fine legs for a woman her age, strappy heels doing nice things to their musculature, her full caboose making the skirt twitch.

Warm applause greeted her, and she did "But Not For Me," and I sat wondering how I'd managed to muff it so bad. Here we'd been having this nice friendly conversation, and I reflexively gave her the vet medicine cover story, before realizing I had no reasonable segue from that to asking her if she'd introduce me to her husband.

She would want to know why, and I couldn't think of anything that made sense. I doubted Richard Cornell was in the market for animal tranquilizers.

By the time she'd started her next song, "You Do Something to Me," I'd about given up. I figured I should just disappear before her set was over, though snubbing the boss' wife (separated from him or not) was not exactly a great plan, either.

But I'd pretty much decided on skipping, and was maybe three seconds away from slipping out of the booth, when a six-footer slid in opposite.

He was dark-haired with some white coming in on the sideburns, a dark tan, lazy eyes and a smirky mouth, but handsome enough at about forty, attired in pale yellow slacks and a darker yellow-and-black checked sportcoat over a black shirt open a few buttons to display several gold chains and some curly black hair.

"My name's Richard Cornell," he said, and extended a hand. "I run the Paddlewheel. Did you and my wife have a nice talkie-poo?"

FOUR

I shook his hand. He smiled across the booth at me in a fashion that I'm sure fooled a lot of people, but I could see the coldness in the aqua-blue eyes, which were half-lidded and made his gaze seem casual when it was heart-attack serious.

"She's a wonderful singer, your wife," I said.

"Indeed she is." The British accent was light but there, a touch of class that went well with his lilting baritone.

"Friendly, too. But I don't want you to get the wrong idea, Mr. Cornell."

He leaned back, smiled on half his face. He'd blinked maybe three times since sitting down. "Angela's a big girl. We're separated. She goes her way and I go mine . . . though I maintain an interest in her welfare. Didn't get your name."

"Jack Gibson," I said.

Cornell folded his arms and the smile

widened, though it had no warmth. "And what brings you to my part of the world, Mr. Gibson?"

Not *this* part of the world — *his* part of the world.

In about half a second I processed the following: he wouldn't have sat down casually to chat up a stray Paddlewheel patron, and as a nearly ex-husband he had no reason to check up on or protect his wife, meaning he was (for whatever reason) suspicious about me, I'd been noticed somehow, and if I trotted out the veterinary meds schtick right now, I'd soon be dancing in the parking lot with two or three of his satin-vest bully boys before he even got around to blinking again.

"Are you always this attentive to your guests, Mr. Cornell?"

A black waitress in an Afro wig delivered him three fingers of what looked to be Scotch over two ice cubes. He smiled, said, "Thank you, darlin' . . . drinky-poo, Mr. Gibson?"

"No thanks."

"That'll be all, darlin'," he told her, kissed the air in her direction and she smiled and walked off.

He watched with admiration, his smile genuine now. "Boobs like cannonballs," he said, and shook his head, eyes darting up.

"You believe it? Wants to be a grade-school teacher. Mine were all prunes."

"Community college student, huh?"

He gave me a sharp look and said, "You pick up a lot, don't you, Mr. Gibson? . . . What were we talking about?"

"I was asking what I'd done to deserve the massa's attention."

He chuckled at that. "You're here alone. You've been here since around nine-thirty. You've had a meal, alone, you gambled alone . . . about broke even I believe, very modest, very controlled . . . you spent some time upstairs, but didn't dance, and you haven't been drinking at all, except possibly a beer and maybe a few gallons of diet cola . . . really, how can you *stand* that bilge?" He shuddered. "Finally you wound up here in the bar, where you struck up a conversation with my wife. In fact, you struck up a lot of conversations this evening."

Either I was getting sloppy, or his security team was smarter than they looked.

"I didn't see any cameras," I said.

That pleased him so much all his teeth came out to play in a beaming smile. "I don't have security cameras — I just have a staff that looks out for their boss. The injuns send up smoke signals to their chiefy-

75

poo, if somebody doesn't fit any of the usual molds."

"More like squaws — with the exception of your no-neck squad, it's mostly women here . . . like Cannonball Katie over there."

His smile settled down and his eyes almost shut as he sipped the Scotch. He reached over for his wife's purse and helped himself to a Virginia Slims — confident enough in his masculinity to risk the estrogen content. He used her matches and got his going, not bothering to ask me if I wanted one. The reports on me probably said I hadn't been smoking. He knew everything about me. He thought.

"Here's the thing, sport," he said, and if condescension were a liquid he would have been dripping. "Casing the joint won't do you any good. I'll be upping my security team and my precautions will go on high alert status, so you can tell your friends that knocking over the Paddlewheel would be a very, very poor idea."

"Of course it would. You're doing land-office business, sure, which means a good payday for a score. But taking down a place that attracts a Wednesday night crowd like this? Calls for a D-Day Invasion."

He wasn't sure what to make of that. His eyes tightened as he drew in smoke, held it

76

so long it might have been marijuana, and let it out. Even in the dim nightclub light, you could see his face was as cracked and leathery as it was handsome.

Then he said, "Whatever you have in mind, mate, ponder this — I am connected to individuals in Chicago who would not rest until anyone who tried anything against this facility was apprehended. And by apprehended, I mean castrated, fed their genitals and dumped in the river."

"Concrete overshoes?"

"Some fashions never go out of style."

"That'd be the Giardelli family, I suppose."

That surprised him, his nostrils flaring, though the eyes remained half-lidded. He said nothing.

I shook my head, laughed a little. "I'm not an advance man for a plunder squad. Get real, Dickie."

". . . Only my friends call me 'Dickie.' "

"Oh, we're going to be friends. You see, I've done work, off and on, myself for the Giardellis. Checking up on me would be tricky, though, because I worked through a middleman and he's dead now. But I can give you chapter and verse on mutual acquaintances."

He set the cigarette in the glass tray. "If

you're a federal agent, Mr. Gibson, I'm asking you to declare yourself, right now. Or we'll be talking entrapment."

"Oh, we're talking entrapment, all right. Anyway, the fix your Chicago friends put in must go at least up into the lower federal rungs. You don't open up a casino because you have the county sheriff in your pocket. This has to go way higher."

"What kind of middleman?"

He'd been thinking. He might even have figured it out.

"I used to do contract work."

"Used to?"

"Now I'm more in . . . preventive maintenance."

"What kind of . . . preventive maintenance?"

"Helping people like you stay alive."

"Why would I need your help to stay alive?"

"Because *other* people still do contract work."

He was staring at me, the eyes wider now, though more alert than scared. He got it. He followed.

"I'm not wearing a wire," I said. "And I don't have a weapon on me. You can have one of your musclemen frisk me, if they can bend over that far."

He had another sip of the Scotch. And another.

He checked his watch, mumbled to himself, "It's after two. . . ." Then he said, "Maybe we should talk privately."

"Maybe we should," I said.

The "after two" reference had been about the dance club on the upper floor closing at that time. He mentioned on the way up in a private elevator off the kitchen that he had a small business office on the restaurant level, but a larger, more comfortable one shared the third floor with the Paddlewheel Lounge.

Office wasn't really the word for it — bachelor pad would be more like it, a room wider than it was long with the far wall engulfed by a projection TV screen and a viewing area consisting of a plump brown leather sofa bookended by overstuffed brown leather chairs. Between them was a glass coffee table under which the projection TV unit lurked, and a brown geometric-patterned area rug was beneath all those furnishings. The exposed floor was a gray marble-like tile, with the upper reaches of the brick walls at left and right given to shelving, books at left, video cassettes and CDs at right; stereo speakers rode the walls, as did track lighting.

The wall to the left of the projection screen displayed a framed Warhol "Marilyn" pop-art print. An open door to the screen's right provided a glimpse of a bedroom, though the lights were off and its shape remained vague. Much less vague was the shape of the slender little blonde, with an Orphan Annie head of yellow curls, who was in sheer white panties, her knees on the rug in front of one brown comfy chair, as she leaned prayerfully over the glass table, snorting a line of coke. And I don't mean Diet.

"Chrissy!" Cornell snapped. "Go wait in the other room."

Still on her knees, she looked up, powder on her nostrils; she was cute as cotton candy, if you injected cotton candy. No more than twenty, I'd guess, skinny enough for her ribs to show but with pert little puffy-nippled handful titties.

"Sure, Dickie," she said.

But she finished snorting before jumping up to pad into the bedroom, displaying a cute dimpled ass and not one iota of cellulite (or for that matter shame), shutting the door tight behind her.

"Sorry," he said.

I shrugged. "Kids."

There was a wet bar against the back wall, next to where we'd come in.

"Drinky?" he asked.

"I'm fine."

He got himself a few inches of Dewar's on the rocks, then gestured to the chair Chrissy had been kneeling before. I took it. It was warm. From here I could see on the glass the ghosts of two more lines of consumed coke. People and their vices.

He seated himself on the brown comfy chair opposite, rested an ankle on a knee — he was wearing Italian loafers and, like me, no socks. It was like we were long-lost brothers — this was just like my place at Paradise Lake, except for the dope, the near-naked doper girl, the projection TV and the leather furniture.

His eyes at half-mast but his smile full-bore, he asked, "So who the fuck are you, love?"

"I'm using Jack Gibson. When I worked for a guy called the Broker, I used Quarry."

His eyes tightened. "I, uh . . . know that name."

"Quarry?"

"No. The Broker. Quad Cities, isn't it?"

"Right. You ever have occasion to use his services?"

"No. Indeed not. But I was . . . *aware* of

81

those services."

"Yeah, well. I used to perform that kind of service. I perform another one now."

He took in some Dewar's, swirled it around, sent it down. "And what service would that be?"

"I have a method, which is my own concern, of following assassins to their intended targets. The assassins usually work in pairs of two — back-up slash recon, and the actual trigger puller."

He pretended to smile on half his face; the rest of his sour puss told the truth. "You sound like Mario Puzo suffering from the D.T.'s. What kind of fantasy *is* this?"

"Not the good kind. Somebody wants you dead, Dickie. I don't know who that somebody is, although I might be able to find out. That would be extra, of course."

"Extra. Extra to what?"

"To the price of saving your ass."

He thought about that. "How would you go about saving my . . . ass?"

"I'd stop the hit from going down."

"Non-violently?"

"Of course not. I'll have to kill the bastards. What do you think?"

His eyes widened and his smile widened and he played at thinking this was funny. "You are a card, Mr. Quarry."

"Let's stick with Gibson. There's no extra charge for the amusement factor."

He grunted a laugh. "This may be the most outrageous shakedown I've ever heard of. You come in to my place of business and make a few references to low people in high places, to convince me of your authenticity . . . and then you presume to have me pay you off, to protect me from what? From *whom?*"

"I'll want twenty thousand dollars," I said, ignoring most of that. "*After* I've delivered. I don't expect you to pay in cash, though with the casino you probably could. But I understand the accounting problems that might ensue."

"Oh you do. Accounting problems."

"I'll give you the banking information — I'm using the Cayman Islands now — and you can have the twenty K transferred to an account there."

"I see. I agree to pay you, and nothing happens to me." He laughed loud enough now for it to ping off the brick wall opposite. "This *has* to be the most *audacious* extortion scheme I've ever heard of . . . and I've heard of a few."

"Bet you have."

His face seemed to darken further under the leathery tan. He slammed the empty tumbler down on the glass and leaned forward and pointed a finger at me. "Listen, booby — you know not with whom you fuck. I ran key clubs on the West End for the Kray brothers when you were sucking your mama's titty."

"I'm a bottle baby."

"I've seen things undreamed of in your fucking philosophy, Horatio. Fuck! I ran Rush Street Clubs for the Giardellis when you were —"

"Shooting gooks with a sniper rifle?"

That stopped him.

"Listen," I said, and I held my hands up, palms open. "I've invested some time and money and energy in this, but I'm well aware it's a speculative endeavor. You can say no — you don't have to buy my Fuller brushes, you can pass on my Amway products, you don't even have to buy any magazine subscriptions to send me to Bible camp. Your choice. Of course, you'll be dead, this time tomorrow."

I rose.

He looked up at me. I had a feeling he had a gun stuffed down in that chair, particularly because of the way his hand was way back on the cushion. If he made a move, I could have the glass coffee table in his face faster than Chrissy could snort a line.

But he raised his own palms and patted the air, gently. "Sit," he said. "Sit."

I sat.

"Suppose I take you seriously," he said. He got a cigarette going, taking one from a gold box on the coffee table — not a Virginia Slim, I'd wager. "Suppose I accept this outrageous scenario as potentially real and not just ridiculous twaddle."

"Isn't twaddle inherently ridiculous?"

He closed his eyes. "You are insufferable."

"Sorry. Just trying to lighten the mood."

"What do you know about this?"

"About this?"

"About how I would be . . . eliminated."

I shrugged. "It's going to be nasty. You're going to be run down by a car."

His eyes popped. "You said something about triggers being pulled. . . ."

"That was meant to cover the whole panorama of how many ways your ass can be 'eliminated.' My guess is, this particular specialist has been brought in so that your death can pass as accidental. Somebody wants you dead who doesn't want a killing coming back on them."

He frowned, looked off toward the door. But he wasn't thinking about Chrissy, I didn't think.

Then his leathery puss turned toward me and he said, slowly, "I *know* who hired this done."

"Ah. So it *is* credible, then."

He nodded. "Very credible. That's why we're still talking, Mr. Quarry."

I didn't correct him. It was his way of saying he was talking to a hired killer, not a veterinary medicine salesman.

"What," he said, "if I wanted that party removed. By that I mean, the party who wanted *me* removed."

"Party of the first part?" I said and risked a grin. "It is a contract, after all. . . . I'd be glad to. I couldn't quote a price until I knew more of the circumstances, but I'd be fine with that."

Really fine — after all, when you kill the contract killers, the guy who hired them might be miffed with you. So eliminating the buyer would be the best kind of contract to get — lucrative and self-interested.

"Should we discuss it?" he asked.

"Let's discuss you. First things first. How many on your security staff?"

"Twelve."

"I counted six."

"Six working tonight."

"Are you including the parking-lot

86

deputy?"

"No."

"Is he trustworthy, the deputy?"

"Of course not."

"So what's the story on law enforcement in Haydee's Port?"

"There isn't any, Mr. Quarry. There's a county sheriff's sub-station in Burris, which is ten miles from Haydee's. They have half a dozen deputies and one very corrupt sheriff. All of them work for not only me but the other businesses in Haydee's."

"Like the Lucky Devil downtown?"

"That's right. The Lucky Devil and all of the other low-rent dives."

"When does the deputy go off duty?"

"You mean, off duty here?"

"Right — when does he stop babysitting your parking lot?"

"He'll stay till the lot's emptied out."

"Which is?"

"Five-fifteen."

"Latest he could still be around?"

"Five-thirty."

"What's your pattern? Do you stay here? You've got a bedroom."

"Not usually. Sometimes on weekends, when I allow myself a little . . . latitude. Otherwise I maintain regular hours."

"So, during the week, when do you leave

here? And where do you go?"

"I leave, oh, about five-thirty or six. I live just down the road a few minutes."

"What about . . . ?" I was nodding toward the closed bedroom door.

"I don't take my work home with me," he said. "I'm separated, and my wife and I don't live together right now, but, still, I wouldn't insult her like that."

He would fuck a little coke slut the floor above where she was singing her heart out, though. Good thing this guy had that English accent or I might think he was a shitheel.

"So when you leave at five-thirty or six, is the lot generally empty?"

"I'm the last out, yes."

"Okay. Makes sense."

"You mean . . . that's when he'd *do* it? He'd . . . Jesus fucking . . . he'd run me down in my own parking lot?"

"Bingo."

"How in God's name is that not suspicious?"

"It's a not a bullet in the head. It's a guy who got run down in the parking lot of a place that serves drinks till dawn. Getting tire tracks on you from a drunk under those conditions isn't suspicious at all, particularly in a county where the sheriff and his deputies are just possibly on the takey-poo."

He thought about that. He was trying to go pale under the tan, and it was damn near working.

"Dickie, how subtle do I have to be about this?"

He blinked at me. The fucker *could* blink, after all. "Subtle?"

"Yeah. If I shoot this prick, will we have the law to answer to? If we have a dead body on our hands, one with a bullet or two in him, can you have him removed?"

He twitched a frown. "If a deputy shows up, we could handle it. Could be expensive. I mean, it would be right out in the open. You saying, if he was behind the wheel of his car, and you shot him, and we had a car with a bullet hole in the windshield and —"

"A driver with a bullet in his head, could you deal with it?"

He flinched. "Is there another way?"

"Might be. Might be."

We both just sat there a while.

"You're asking a lot," he said.

"I know."

"You come in with this wild story. It's credible, in its way, and yet it's fantastic."

"I know."

"Is there someone I could call?"

"You mean do I have references?"

"I guess that was a stupid question."

"Well . . . funny thing is, I did a job like this for the guy who used to own this place. I was never here before — I met him at a much smaller operation, in Des Moines. Frank Tree. Did you buy this place from him?"

"No. I heard of him — he's the guy who opened the Paddlewheel, turned it from a warehouse into a goldmine. It came to me through my Chicago friends. Gave me and my wife a chance to buy in. They're silent partners."

"Yeah. Silent until they get noisy." I stood. "Come with me."

"Where?"

"Just out to your parking lot."

He looked alarmed. "Why, is *he* out there?"

"No! Hell, no. He'll be anywhere but there."

Truth was, I didn't know the details of Monahan's approach. I couldn't imagine he would use the Buick he'd bought in Des Moines for the job. How would he get back? Call a fucking cab?

Actually, he probably *could* ditch the car at the scene and walk to somewhere and call a cab and then take the train or a bus home or anyway a bus to an airport

90

where . . .

Fuck it. Those details weren't important. Stopping him was. And convincing Cornell to *let* me stop him. I was almost there with Dickie boy. Just needed to close the sale.

In the elevator, I said, "What's the story about that farmhouse across the way?"

"That? Farmer sold out to one of those big corporate farms, maybe ten years ago, everything but the house itself and a small plot of land. He and his wife lived in that goddamn hovel, and then after his wife died, the farmer stayed on himself. He finally did the world the courtesy of dying, and about four months ago, I bought the property. We'll build a hotel over there, as soon as all the right wheels have been greased. We'd need to buy some of that expensive farm land around there to . . . why in the world are you asking?"

"That's where the back-up guy has been staking you out, probably for a couple weeks."

"The hell!"

"The hell," I said with a nod.

Soon I'd led him out into his own parking lot and over to my Sunbird. I got around behind and used the key to open the trunk and let him have a look at the fetus-curled blond kid. The blood on him was black and crusty now and he was very white; it made him look even blonder, too clean-cut for the Poison t-shirt. Lots of blood turned to crunchy-looking black had pooled and dried on the trunk floor.

"What is it you guys call it," I said. "The boot?"

"Fuck *me.* Who's this?"

"The back-up guy. I took him out on spec."

"Christ." He looked at me with a ghastly, melting-wax expression; his face had managed to go white despite the tan, finally. "What the hell's *this* going to cost me?"

"It's like drugs — first one's free. Ask your little girlfriend about it." I shut the lid. "Well?"

"Twenty K it is."

We went back inside to talk some more.

FIVE

A line of trees defined the far end of the Paddlewheel parking lot, the moonlight a memory now, the sky doing its darkest-before-the dawn routine. Around four-thirty A.M., I nosed the Sunbird into a slot next to the river in the last row of spaces, flush against those trees. The lot was still about half-full, the deputy parked four spaces down, where he'd backed in to better fulfill his security duties.

A trick of surveillance is to sit in the back seat and — since the deputy was asleep — he didn't notice me get out and make the shift to the rear.

The lot had four light poles, two on either side, and was rather under-illuminated, which helped me blend into the darkness of the back seat. I got comfortable. I'd made a run back to the motel and was now in black — black t-shirt, black jeans, black socks, black running shoes, even my fucking underwear was black. All it would have taken for full commando was some black smeared under my eyes, but I didn't go overboard. Also, I couldn't risk black gloves, because that would stand out in this summer weather, whereas the black attire could otherwise be just a fashion choice.

By four-forty-five, the lot had cleared out. Most of those heading for their cars were flat out staggering, and I was glad I wasn't going to be out on the road with them where it was dangerous. Not that Deputy Fife paid the obvious drunks any heed. At least he'd woken up when a slamming car door had delivered him a wake-up call.

By five-fifteen, the deputy was gone and the lot had cleared out but for a dozen cars toward my end — employee cars — and waitresses and satin-vested security guys and other workers came staggering out, too, presumably not drunk, just night-shift beat. As these cars were pulling out, Monahan in his green Buick Regal glided in, and backed into the deputy's now vacant space.

He didn't glance my way — the employee cars were all down at this end, even Cornell's (a navy-blue Corvette), so Monahan surely assumed the Sunbird was one of those. I was slouched in back, and I doubted he'd made me. He probably wouldn't recognize the Sunbird, either — if he'd paid that much attention to me, he would either have bailed by now or dealt with me over at the Wheelhouse.

No, I wasn't on the prick's radar. I'd bet my life on it. Not a figure of a speech.

Pretty soon, if Richard Cornell was staying true to his pattern, he would be exiting the Paddlewheel and loping all the way across the lot to his Corvette, making long shadows as dawn presented itself. Monahan would hit the gas, work up some speed, and pretend to be heading for the exit down by the building, but would swerve and smack Cornell like a bug on a windshield. If this didn't clearly kill Cornell, Monahan would back up and make sure a wheel crushed the mark's head.

Then Monahan would be gone, headed somewhere to dump the vehicle.

But Cornell wouldn't be coming out of that building, not any time soon, at least. And I knew that if I didn't make my move soon — before it got suspicious that the Paddlewheel's impresario wasn't sticking to his pattern — then the Vehicular Homicide specialist would hightail.

This wasn't a science. I could only predict so much. But Monahan wouldn't be here if he'd checked in with his blond back-up man, or I should say tried to check in with him. As far as Monahan likely knew, the blond kid was somewhere over near that farmhouse, watching his partner's back. My sense was that I was on top of this thing.

So I went into my act.

I played at waking up in the back seat, yawning and blinking and rubbing my face, like a drunk who'd crawled back there to sober up and had just come around, now that rosy-fingered dawn had slapped him awake.

I got out of the Sunbird's back seat with all the subtlety of a street mime, making sure the nine millimeter Browning nudging my spine didn't show. I came around as if to get in front, behind the wheel, then paused and looked right at Monahan, seated behind his own wheel, and squinted, and grinned, as if noticing an old, dear friend.

Staggering some, I headed right for him, not quickly; his window was down and his bland insurance salesman's face was turned my way, the expression blank but the eyes tight with irritation and perhaps, yes, suspicion.

"My *pool* buddy!" I said, sloppily, holding out my arms and hands like Jolson singing "Mammy." "Pal! You got a sec?"

He said, "What?" Seldom in the history of

mankind has that word been uttered with less enthusiasm.

I leaned against his car like a drive-in waitress. "I tried to sleep it off, dude, but I am still drunker than shit. Can I hitch a ride to the motel? Pretty please?"

This was delivered in an imitation drunk fashion, not as broad as Foster Brooks, but I was pushing it.

He looked up at me coldly, then turned his face toward his windshield. He nodded toward the road. "I'm waiting for somebody. It's not that far. You can —"

He was probably going to say, "Walk it," but we'll never know, because I reached a hand in behind his head and slammed his forehead into his steering wheel. It didn't knock him out, much less kill him, but stunned him enough to give me time to take the nine millimeter out of my back waistband, gripped by the barrel, and swing it around like a hammer.

It was a good swing. The butt crushed bone like crisp fresh celery snapping and sank in deep enough to bring back blood and brains. He flopped onto the rider's seat, which put him out of view except for me and maybe God, and was a good thing.

I leaned in the window and wiped the gun off on his green polo shirt, gore and prints, then opened his rear door and tossed the weapon on the floor.

Then I went back over to my Sunbird, got in and started it up, and backed it around so that the two cars made an L putting my tail as close as possible to his, which made for a quick transfer of the dead stiff (and the blond kid was very stiff now) from my trunk into his.

I moved my Sunbird back to where it had been, then (in black leather driving gloves now) returned to the Buick Regal and shoved Monahan's corpse over to make room behind the wheel. Except for the smell of shit — Monahan had evacuated on dying, and I don't mean escaped from the car — it went fairly slick. Maybe two and a half minutes had passed between my asking for a ride and my climbing behind his wheel.

After buckling up and getting all the windows down, to get some fucking air in and make the stench more tolerable, I pulled out and soon was on the old two-lane highway along the river, which at this hour was deader than Monahan. The sun was still low when I pulled over where the curving road had just this little gravel apron where you could stop and get out and take in the beautiful Mississippi river view. I did this. The river was so orange with dawn, it was damn near red. I had a look at the drop-off into the trees that lined the riverbank — you couldn't see the bottom. Must have been five, six hundred feet.

I stood there waiting and listening but nothing human or mechanical touched my ears — just nature sounds, birds and the rush of water and maybe a distant dog bark. I got in the Buick and drove it to where the front tires were almost over. Then I got out again, reached in and shoved the gear shift into drive and ducked back before the vehicle took me with it.

Then the Buick and Monahan and the blond kid in the trunk were flying faster than the motor was taking them. The first loud sounds were trees breaking up and leaves getting ripped apart but the explosion blotted that out, the balloon of orange and red and yellow jumping up above the trees, then immediately dissipating, which was good. I'd have hated to see all those trees go. There was another road down there, and with any luck some rural volunteer fire department would get there in time to help out Mother Nature. Monahan and the blond kid were past it.

I walked down the bluff to the little picnic area where I'd been told to wait, and it felt longer, but only four minutes had passed before the sporty little red Subaru stopped to pick me up.

I got in and looked over at the woman behind the wheel.

"I heard it," Angela Dell said, looking pale and older in the early morning light. "My God, it sounded horrible."

"It looked fine," I said. "Take me to the motel. Want some breakfast?"

She had coffee. We were in the same rear booth where Monahan and the kid had schemed, yesterday, though she didn't know that. The irony was mine alone to savor, but I wasn't bothering, being more interested in the scrambled egg skillet and pancakes.

Back at the Paddlewheel, last night — or actually, this morning, but in the early pre-dawn hours — I'd asked Cornell if there was anyone he could trust.

We were still in his bachelor-pad office.

"I trust my wife," he said.

"I mean somebody reliable who wouldn't mind getting their hands a little messy — second-hand, but messy. I want to get rid of this guy, who's coming to run you down, in a way that won't come back on you."

"What do you have in mind?"

I told him if I shot the fucker, we'd have a dead guy — actually two dead guys, count-

100

ing the blond kid — in the Paddlewheel parking lot to either explain or get rid of. I said that if I could stop the guy but leave him and his buddy in the remains of what seemed to be an automobile accident, that would be less likely to come back to him. With all the after-hours drinking going on in Haydee's, there had to be the occasional drunk-driving death around here.

"Yes," Cornell said, nodding, eyes narrow in thought, "and I know just the place to stage it. You'd have to drive forty miles, but it would put it in the next county, far enough away to provide a cushion."

"Yeah, a cushy-poo would be good," I said.

"Are you making sport of me?"

"Think of it as good-natured fun, and not mean-spirited ridicule. What I need is a ride back, and I'd rather not have it be you. I wouldn't think your wife would want to be part of covering up killings. Anyway, your marriage is on the skids, isn't it?"

He waved that off. "Our marriage is over, but our business thrives. And we're heading into a whole new era for the Paddlewheel and Haydee's Port, and she will benefit right along with me."

"For now, skip the future-plans stuff. I met her, and she's a nice woman. Don't you have some flunky who —"

"Can blackmail my ass till eternity and a weekend? No thank you. She's no angel, my Angela. You know what her maiden name was?"

"Something that shortens to 'Dell.' "

"It shortens there from Giardelli. Her father is Anthony Giardelli."

"No shit?"

"None."

Which explained what Cornell's Chicago connections were, and in part what role Angela had played in getting the Paddlewheel up and running. I had done jobs for the Giardellis. I'd also killed Anthony Giardelli's brother Lou, once upon a time, but that was neither here nor there. No one knew that but me.

"What will you tell her, Dickie?"

"That you're a troubleshooter who works outside the law. That I brought you in to take care of some assholes sent by the competition to eliminate me. She won't want any details."

"Good. And she'd do this for you?"

"For the business. Also . . ." He shrugged, and his smile was a white slash in his deeply tanned face. ". . . she still loves me."

I shrugged. "What's not to love?"

Now we were having breakfast, Angela and me, or anyway I was having breakfast

102

and she was having coffee.

"Listen," I said, "I'm sorry about lying to you last night. About being a salesman and all."

She shook her head. She had a dazed, distant expression. "That was your cover story. I understand." She shivered, and sipped coffee to stave off the cold; the air conditioning in the Wheelhouse was going pretty hard. Very quietly she said, "How many?"

"How many what?"

"How many people were in that car?"

"Two."

"Both were sent to . . . hurt Dickie?"

"Both sent to kill Dickie."

"He'd be dead if . . ."

"If I hadn't stopped it, yes. It wasn't my idea to involve you. I'm sorry."

She shook her head. She was very beautiful, but she did look well-past forty, and every year of it. Minus plastic surgery, a woman could not exist as a nightclub singer without the drinking and smoking and carousing, her own and of those around her, taking a toll.

Still, I found her very attractive. I liked the mix of worldliness and vulnerability, and let's face it, she had a rack to die for, even if it was lost in the sweatshirt half of a purple running suit. Her long reddish-blonde hair was back in a big ponytail, which revealed some of the miles on the nice face, and the grooves in her neck.

"Listen," she said, leaning in, "I *said* I'd help, when Dickie asked, and I did it with my eyes open. We're in a tough business, Dickie and me. How much do you know about what's going on right now in Haydee's? And for that matter, Chicago?"

The restaurant was fairly full — the crowd looked local, including farmers, as we were past the drinking-crowd breakfast of the earlier morning. But I was still concerned about being overhead, though we'd kept it nicely hushed.

"This isn't a come-on," I said, "but if you want to talk, we could have some privacy in my room."

She shrugged. "Let me get another coffee to go."

She did, and I finished the breakfast.

My motel room had a little area with a round table and two chairs, probably designed for businessmen to work, and I sat her and her coffee there. I invited her to watch the television while I showered, and she declined. She said she preferred to sit and think.

I got out of the black clothing I'd done

the killing in, showered and got the sweat and any stray blood or dried gore off me, shaved and generally became human again. I'd brought a fresh pair of black jeans and a light blue polo shirt in the bathroom with me, and I put them on, then padded out barefoot.

I sat across from her. "Sorry to make you wait. I had a long night. I probably ought to get some sleep pretty soon."

She sat up straight. "Oh, I'm sorry, I can —"

"No! I'm fine with your company. I like your company. Anyway, I want to hear what you have to say."

She managed a smile. "I may be out of line getting into any of this. Dickie should probably fill you in, but . . . I don't know why exactly, I just think you have a right to know, before you get in over your head."

That was an interesting remark. She knew I'd just murdered two people, even if she didn't know the details, and yet she didn't think I was in over my head yet.

"Jack . . . it *is* Jack?"

Actually, it wasn't, but she didn't need my real name any more than you do.

"It's Jack."

"Jack, do you know whose daughter I am?"

I nodded. "Your husband told me — Tony Giardelli's girl."

"Right. And you know who *he* is."

"Sure. He and his brother Vincent and their late brother Lou are about as high up in the Chicago Outfit as you can go."

"All right. You know that much. Have you ever worked for the Giardelli interests?"

"From time to time, but not directly."

She nodded. "I understand. My father has always liked to be . . . well-insulated . . . from anything violent or illegal. What you probably don't know is that my father and his brother Vincent are not partners — they each have their own interests, and over the years they've been friendly rivals. Lately . . . not so friendly. It's never been direct, again there's much insulation, but Haydee's Port has become a kind of a breeding ground in the family war that's brewing."

"How so?"

"My father backs me, and Dickie, in the Paddlewheel, maintains a financial interest. It's Papa's belief, a belief fostered by my husband, that the future of Haydee's Port is upscale. This Wild West wide-open downtown doesn't mine the full potential of Haydee's, taking money from drunks and bilking the blue-collar crowd. And it's dangerous, the kind of *eyesore* that at some

106

point the politicians could be pressured into removing."

"Whereas," I said, "the classier Paddle-wheel can be a Midwestern Las Vegas, where everybody wink-winks at the illegal side of it."

"If Dickie has his way, with a new hotel, and beyond that plans to refurbish and reinvent downtown Haydee's Port, we might see gambling become legal, in this county anyway . . . and it could truly become, as you say, a Midwestern Vegas."

"What do you think of that plan?"

"I think it's brilliant. I think I'll be very wealthy in my golden years, and I'll probably have a place to practice my art for as long as I want."

"I wouldn't think you'd need the Paddle-wheel to have a singing career. Between your talent, and your daddy's connections —"

She had stopped me with a raised palm. "No. I don't want to travel, and I don't want to be beholden to Papa."

"You already are. Didn't your Papa make the Paddlewheel possible?"

"Of course he did. But my talent, and Dickie's business sense, and vision, have taken it to a whole new plateau."

"Okay. But there's a problem, right? Uncle Vince?"

She shrugged. "Hard to say whether it's coming directly from Vince or if it's the Lucky Devil crowd, causing trouble for Dickie, knowing they have the tacit approval of their Chicago backer."

"Who are the Lucky Devil crowd?"

"The old man who owns virtually every bar, strip club and brothel downtown is Gigi Giovanni. He was thick with Uncle Vince back in the '40s and '50s, came with Vince's blessing and backing to Haydee's Port, in the early '60s. He's kind of a recluse, and has turned most of the responsibility over to his son, Jerry G. My guess would be, any trouble that's been sent Dickie's way, comes from Jerry G, not his father."

"Why do you say that?"

"Jerry G is ambitious, and he's a hothead. He's a sadistic son of a bitch and he's a god-damn cheat and he drinks and dopes more than any of his customers and breaks in all the young girls before putting them to work on their backs."

"Any bad qualities?"

That made her smile. "Nothing much fazes you, does it?"

"No."

"You've heard what you've gotten yourself

into, and you don't mind?"

"I won't mind if the money is right. I'll have to talk to your husband."

"We keep referring to Dickie as my husband . . . and he is my husband. But we *are* separated."

"Right."

"You mind if I turn off the lights?"

"No."

She rose, and went over and turned off the lights and I sat at the table and waited while she went into the bathroom and took her own shower. When the bathroom door opened, the light was behind her and the front of her was in blue-gray shadow. She was voluptuous and those breasts were full with nipples that were erect and thick and long and a deep pink against very pale flesh. Her pubic bush was thick and dark, her thighs a little fleshy. She was no kid.

But she knew what she was doing when she knelt in front of me, where I sat, and opened my trousers, unzipped me and got my already erect cock out to have a look at it.

"I want to thank you for what you did for my husband," she said.

"Okay," I said, and felt myself slip into the warmth of her mouth.

She brought me almost to climax and I

swear I was cross-eyed when she took me by the hand like mommy leading baby, assuming baby had his trousers around his ankles, and all but shoved me onto the bed, where she climbed on top of me and took my dick up into a warm, tight place and ground her hips into me and ground them some more and I watched hypnotized by the swaying fruit of those breasts, reaching my mouth out to grab at them, like a child on a merry-go-round going for the brass ring, and when she came, she came so hard her eyes rolled back in her head.

I came so hard my eyes uncrossed.

She flopped off beside me, breathing hard. I was breathing hard, too.

"You're welcome," I said.

She nuzzled my neck, then got up and her round, dimpled bottom receded into the bathroom, where the door closed, and I was left in darkness, to ponder the character of a woman who didn't want to divorce her cheating husband because she was Catholic, but was fine with covering up killings for him as well as fucking the help by way of showing her appreciation for a job well done.

But then I'd never really understood women.

Six

I parked the Sunbird on the street between a pick-up truck and a row of Harleys. It was eight P.M. in beautiful downtown Haydee's Port, and not really hopping yet, though the seven or eight bars on one side of the street and the eight or nine bars on the other were spilling red and blue and green and yellow neon onto the sidewalks along with loud music from country to heavy metal, frat rock to New Wave. The neon spillage made a sort of blurry melted rainbow but the melding of popular music was just plain noise.

Smoke and beer smell issued from every entryway, both invitation and threat, though it was too early for the bouquet of puke. Guys in groups of two or three or four swaggered along the sidewalk, window-shopping for just the right bar, but no similar groups of women were on the prowl.

I'd been told that early evening in Haydee's Port was slow, but that it picked up from ten till maybe one and then stayed steady, although the crowd gradually shifted from those looking for wide-open fun to seekers of a bar that served alcohol after one A.M., closing time across the river.

The Lucky Devil was no classier than any other dive along Main Street, just bigger, taking up three storefronts, the right and left ones with front windows painted black. The center storefront allowed you to see into a dingy bar, and the only promise of something special were two signs in the window — one a big, bold red-and-black cartoon outlined in red neon of a grinning, winking devil's head, right down to the regulation pointy mustache and beard; the other a red cursive blinking neon spelling out the establishment's name.

I went through double-push doors into a space about the size of a high-school cafeteria and every bit as inviting. The front half of the smoky chamber was a drab collection of red-plastic-covered tables with old-fashioned wooden chairs, and (at the bar itself) stools whose red seat cushions were bursting. Behind the bartender, shelves of booze were back-lit red, but then the whole room was dimly lit and red-tinged, with beer-sign halos spotted around. The lighting was better at the rear, where up a few steps behind pipe railing, four pool tables under Schlitz chandeliers were all in use by guys in plaid shirts with rolled-up sleeves open to either white t-shirts or bare chests. They were either hicks or gay. Or gay hicks.

The joint was encased in the cheapest paneling known to God or man or even your Uncle Phil, beautified by black-marker graffiti that made dating and other suggestions. Right now the tables were about half full, and the bar about the same. The clientele appeared to be blue-collar or below, displaying lots of frayed, faded jeans, a look courtesy of factory work, not factory fabrication. One corner had been taken over by bikers in well-worn leathers — the bikers were pretty well-worn themselves, in their thirties or forties. Marlon Brando in *The Wild One* had been a long fucking time ago.

I was overdressed in my navy t-shirt and black jeans and running shoes, but nobody seemed to notice. I took one of the open stools at the bar and ordered whatever was on tap, and asked a few questions of the bartender, a guy in a blue-striped white shirt with rolled-up sleeves over a black t-shirt; he had black wavy hair and a thick black mustache, and looked a little like Tom Selleck's dumber, not-so-good-looking brother.

"So where's all this famous action I keep hearing about?" I asked pleasantly.

"What kind you looking for?"

"I keep an open mind."

He leaned an elbow against the bar. "The girls over at those tables have trailers either side of the parking lot."

Four girls in lots of makeup and with a plentitude of high feathered hair and a modicum of spandex dress were at a table smoking and staring at nothing, unless maybe they were playing invisible cards. They had drinks in tumblers that might have been whiskey but probably were tea. They looked like prom queens, if this were prom night in Hades, which it kind of was.

"Trailers out back, huh? What does twenty-five bucks get you?"

"Their attention. Now, if you're interested in a game of chance, you'll want to head that-a-way."

The bartender gestured to a doorless doorway to the right of where the pool table level rose, presumably providing passage to the adjacent storefront. A brawny black guy in a black polo with a red cursive *Lucky Devil* on the breast and black jeans was seated on a wooden chair on a boxy platform, like a low-riding lifeguard station. Or maybe he was just waiting for the right white guy to come along to give him a shoeshine. In any case, he was keeping watch on the bar and standing guard on that door, his arms folded like a genie; somehow I didn't think he was granting wishes.

I finished my beer and wandered over there. I paused in front of the big black lifeguard and looked up at him, and asked, "Okay I go on in?"

"You free, white and twenty-one, ain't you?"

I decided this was a rhetorical question, and went on through. I expected to find the casino, but did not — this was another bar, but with a big hardwood dance floor, lightly sawdusted, with a stage that butted up where the front window was blacked out. Under hot colored lights, four guys in cowboy hats and tattered t-shirts and jeans and boots were getting ready to play. The tables were only maybe a third full. It was so early the males and females were still in their own little enclaves.

This seemed a different clientele than next door, and was not that different from the dance crowd at the Paddlewheel Lounge. The age was twenties and early thirties, the male attire running from denim jackets to Hawaiian shirts, parachute pants to designer

115

jeans, the female attire from leopard print tops to vests over tube tops, miniskirts to short shorts. A girl of maybe twenty-five in a black-and-yellow backless minidress, with high heels and a yard-in-all-directions of frizzy blonde hair twitched her taut tail as she headed from the ladies' room back to her hive of half a dozen honeys.

I bought another beer and sat at the bar and watched as the band began to play Southern Rock at ear-bleed level, and waitresses in low-cut spandex minidresses took orders and not very discreetly dealt drugs. This section of the Lucky Devil had the same shitty wall paneling, but framed Patrick Nagel beauties and movie posters (*Flashdance, For Your Eyes Only*) indicated a vague sense of purpose if not style.

At the rear another bouncer perched on a lifeguard stand, a white guy this time, also in a Lucky Devil polo shirt — a bruiser with a nose that had been broken so many times you couldn't really call it a nose anymore, and eyes that weren't missing anything. Next to him were push-through doors, and patrons of various stripes had been cutting through to those doors, opening them to reveal glimpses of a bustling casino beyond.

I watched as the males and females began to intermingle — when they weren't going off independently for a toot or what-have-you in the can, anyway — and took in the bar band's respectable covers of ZZ Top, Lynyrd Skynyrd and 38 Special, and made the beer last a good hour. This bartender was a skinny good-natured kid with thinning hair, a wispy mustache and a khaki shirt over an Alabama tee.

"Seems pretty tame," I said, between songs. "I heard this place ran wild."

"Wild enough. More flavors of sin than Baskin Robbins got ice cream."

"I dunno. Nobody seems that frisky."

He shrugged. "We have some heavy-duty bouncers, dude. Fights don't last long in the Lucky."

"Is the casino a key club or something? Or can any fool go back there?"

"Anybody with a few bucks and a ball or two is welcome."

So I went back there. The casino took up only the back half of that one storefront — not a particularly impressive layout, drab and piddling and bare bones, compared to the Paddlewheel's operation.

Overseen by two more bouncers at stubby lifeguard stands, the smoke-swirled room, with the same crummy wood paneling, had a craps table, a roulette wheel, two blackjack stations, and its own small bar, from which the waitresses in black spandex minidresses picked up their trays of free drinks for the suckers. Along two walls were slot machines, old ones, those squat metal numbers that dated back to the '40s and '50s — no video poker, and no flashy electronic modern numbers. Strictly old-fashioned one-armed bandits.

If the Paddlewheel was today, the Lucky Devil sure seemed like yesterday. The best I could say for them was they were catering to a younger crowd, with their Southern Rock and hot-and-cold running drugs. Otherwise this was pretty sad, as casinos went.

The patrons did not seem particularly well-heeled, at least not at this time of night, which was approaching ten. I saw everybody from farmers to factory workers to college kids, and in that sense the Lucky Devil gambling layout was democracy in action, bib-overalls, plaid shirts and Members Only jackets all voting with their money.

So far, I had seen nobody at the Lucky Devil who looked even vaguely like management. And I'd had a good description from Richard Cornell of both the old man, Gigi, and his son Jerry G.

"Odds of you seeing the old man," Cornell had told me this afternoon, in his smaller, more businesslike second-floor office at the Paddlewheel, "are next to nil. He lives on the third floor of the building, and since his wife died ten years ago, he's a god-damned hermit."

"Why the Howard Hughes routine?"

I was sitting across from him. Cornell, in a yellow sport jacket and orange turtleneck, was seated behind a big black metal desk in the surprisingly functional office. He was drinking coffee and I had a can of Diet Coke.

"It may be sorrow for the loss of Mrs. Giovanni," Cornell said, "but I doubt it, since he's always been a womanizing son of a bitch. He has everything he wants up there, it's a lavishly appointed apartment, I understand. He's in his seventies and they send up girls when he's so inclined, and he has a full-time chef. There's a satellite dish near the parking lot, so he can watch sports and naked women and anything he likes. Why leave?"

"What about Jerry G?"

"Young Jerry is fairly hands-on. He also has an apartment spanning the second floor over several of the dives. You should see him on the floor of the casino, however, and possibly elsewhere at the Lucky Devil, unless he's in one of his poker games."

"Tell me about those."

"There's a very high-stakes game in a room in back — not part of the casino, if you can call that hellhole a casino. It's not every night — depends on Jerry's whim, and the availability of players who can afford it. You see, it's strictly for the big boys — buy-in is a grand. You don't have ten grand to throw around, don't bother sitting down."

"Crooked?"

"I don't think so. Not that Jerry G isn't a confirmed cheater, as a casino manager — I think you'll find the gaming rigged for the house. But Jerry G takes pride in his poker playing. He thinks he's a world-class player. And he's done well in Vegas competitions, truth be told."

"You wouldn't have ten grand in cash around, would you?"

The aqua eyes in the heavily tanned face regarded me coldly, though he was working the smile on me, by way of distraction. "I already wired twenty thousand to your Cayman Islands account," he said. "Would this be an advance, or . . . ?"

"It would be your money. If I lose it, it's gone."

"And if you win?"

"You get the ten grand back."

He chuckled. "And doesn't *that* sound

fair? Mr. Quarry, you are a cheeky devil. A regular card."

"Cards sound like they may be the best way in for me, with Jerry G." I shifted in my chair. "We haven't talked about exactly what you want done."

"No we haven't."

"You'd like me to remove whoever it was that hired that contract on you."

"Yes."

"And you're convinced it's either the father, Gigi Giovanni, or the son, Jerry G."

He nodded. "Or possibly both. In concert."

"So, do you want me to determine which it was?"

"Could you do that?"

"Possibly. Could be tricky. But might be possible."

"What's the alternative?"

I shrugged. "Just take them both out."

"What would that cost me?"

"Well . . . double."

"Forty thousand."

"I was thinking fifty."

He blinked. Stop the presses. "What's the extra ten for?"

"For killing mob guys. Consider it hazardous duty pay."

"And it's twenty-five if you determine

which G hired the hit, and take care of only him."

"Yes. And that might prove a bargain, as it's maybe the harder job. I have to play undercover cop and snoop around and not get killed doing it. Just popping them both, if I could stage-manage the right circumstances, could be relatively simple. In and out."

The leather of his forehead grew grooves. "The Giovannis have a small army at the Lucky, you know. Bouncers and strongarms. No shortage of muscles and guns. You don't expect me to pay for anybody *else* you have to take care of along the way."

"What, collateral damage? No. That's my problem. I don't charge for soldiers, only generals."

This he found amusing, the leathery flesh around the eyes crinkling with glee. His big white smile seemed genuine. Nice to know he had a sense of humor.

"Dickie," I said, "you're tied in with your wife's father, back in Chicago — Tony Giardelli. I need to know if you've consulted him about this."

He shook his head. "Uncle Tony expects me to take care of my own problems."

"But would he back you up, after the fact?"

"Oh yes. He knows very well what's at stake."

"What *is* at stake?"

That stopped him, and he thought for several long moments, then got up and gestured me to follow him.

Soon we were in his third-floor office-cum-apartment. The little blonde, Chrissy, was in sheer panties and an athletic-style t-shirt with her bottom on the brown leather couch and her bare feet on the coffee table. She was watching *The $25,000 Pyramid,* or anyway it was on — she was lacquering her fingernails, a joint making its musky fragrance known, smoldering in an ashtray, while on the big screen, Dick Clark loomed like an Easter Island statue.

Cornell did not speak to the girl as he led me past the viewing area into the bedroom, where a big round bed was unmade; a mirror was on the ceiling — it would be. The river view from here would have been magnificent, but black curtains blotted it out. He ushered me to a big glass table with black metal legs and gestured to an elaborate architectural model.

"*That's* the future, Mr. Quarry," he said.

And it was, the future of Haydee's Port, anyway. The downtown buildings were intact, but remodeled into a quaint, family-friendly assembly of projected shops, an almost Disneyfied downtown out of the '20s or '30s with a drugstore, ice-cream emporium, movie house, antique shops, restaurants and more. The Lucky Devil and all the other fallen angels were out of business, in this particular future — only the Casey's General Store survived.

And the Paddlewheel, on its part of the mini-overview, now included a five-story hotel where the blond kid's farmhouse currently stood, and a riverboat sat next to the Paddlewheel on the blue strip on the model representing the Mississippi.

"We are very close to legal gambling in Illinois," Cornell said, "a few years away at most. It will likely require that the gambling take place on a state-sanctioned riverboat. And my operation will be ready, with a top-flight resort where couples and families and respectable folks of all sorts can come enjoy the quaint little river town of Haydee's Port."

"You really think you can turn hell into paradise?"

"Haydee's Port wasn't always a den of sin. You know, it was named for fur trader Robert A. Haydee, who established a trading post on the land under us right now, back in 1827."

Somehow I didn't imagine Robert A. had cohabited with a coke-snorting vixen, but then I'm not that up on my history.

But Cornell went on with his sales pitch, letting me know that Haydee's Port had once been a thriving city, home to five thousand God-fearing residents, a port serving the surrounding farming community. God, unimpressed, had sent a flood in 1912 that wiped the town out, and the businesses that were able relocated across the river. What had grown up in its place was the mini-Sin City we all knew and loved, a population of less than two hundred with a dozen bars and two casinos.

I asked him, "You really think the Illinois state government is going to get in bed with the mob?"

"Are you kidding?"

I shrugged. "Yeah. That was pretty dumb."

He beamed down at his little play town. "My wife's father will think I'm the New Improved Jesus if I can find a way to put the Giovannis out of business in Haydee's Port."

"What will Tony's brother Vincent think?"

Cornell shrugged dismissively. "He'll have to go along. The mob backs a winner."

"My understanding is that Tony and Vincent Giardelli are rivals — two godfathers, each looking for a way to topple the other."

"Yes, but they can't go after each other frontally. They're *brothers* — one family member, that high up in That Thing of Theirs, murder the other? No. They can pretend to peacefully co-exist, while trying to undermine each other, yes. But murdering your own blood . . . that just isn't done."

"That must be those family values I keep hearing about."

He gestured to his toy town. "You have to understand, Mr. Quarry — Haydee's Port is a microcosm of the situation in Chicago."

"What's a microcosm?"

"In this case, it's a big struggle reduced to one small battlefield. If I triumph here, Tony's stock rises in Chicago."

"Okay," I said, not giving a shit. "What do you want done?"

"Why don't we start with me giving you ten grand to play in that poker game?"

"What did you say the buy-in was?"

"A thousand."

"I can probably get by on five."

"Good. I have that in my office safe downstairs. Go get the lay of the land, Mr. Quarry, and come back to me with a recommendation."

"You mean, whether to pop pop, or his

kid, or both?"

"You are a man of quiet eloquence, Mr. Quarry."

"Fuckin' A."

So now I was in the dreary Lucky Devil casino, where I lost twenty bucks playing craps but won fifty at blackjack, the dealer of which was a redheaded gal with short permed hair and a trowel of well-arranged makeup on her almost pretty face.

"Is there any poker here?" I asked. I had her to myself at the moment.

She wore a black vest over a white shirt with a black string tie. "There's a private game. Strictly for high rollers."

I decided not to be a jerk and point out that there was no "rolling" in poker, high or low or otherwise, and said, "How much is the buy-in?"

She confirmed it as a thousand and I said, "I can make that happen. How do you make the game happen?"

"Doesn't start till one. Goes all night."

"Define 'all night.' "

"Dawn or so. Usually breaks up around six."

"Just one table?"

"Yeah. The boss himself deals."

"Just deals?"

"No, he plays, too. He says the house

always has an advantage, and his advantage is, he always deals."

"But does he always win?"

"No. It's a straight game. Would I lie to you?"

I showed her a hundred. "Would you?"

She took it. "No. What's your name?"

"Jack Gibson."

"In five minutes, I take a break. You're lucky — Wednesday's the only weeknight there's a game. I'll put your name in then, if there's an opening. I'll let you know."

I played an ancient slot till she came over and said, "You're in," giving me a white chip with a magic-marker checkmark on it. "Go in at quarter till." She nodded toward a door next to one of the lifeguard-stand bouncers.

This meant I had around two hours to kill, and I wanted to relax, so I wandered back through the Southern Rock dance club into the center bar and on through another set of double doors into the Lucky Devil's strip club.

It was pretty basic — the music here, courtesy of an idiot DJ in a booth who was also flashing disco lights over the stage, consisted of relatively current hits — "Talking in Your Sleep" by the Romantics was going right now, and the short busty brunette in a cowboy hat and fringed vest and g-string was into it, working one of two poles on the single long narrow stage around which all the chairs were taken. Males of every variety, except gay, were seated there — young, old, blue-collar, college-kid, bank president, janitor, middle-aged, geezer, you name it, each with dollar in hand, eager for a stripper to come over, rub her tits in his face, and let him deposit the buck in her g-string.

I had no trouble finding a table toward the back. The room was lined in mirrors, which made it seem bigger and also put naked dancing female flesh everywhere, even though there was only one girl on stage at a time. Strippers in g-strings and pasties and feather boas and heels were trolling for guys to give table dances to, but not always succeeding, since that was five bucks not a single.

The girls were all under thirty, most closer to twenty, and seemed a mix of locals (possibly more of that community college talent) and gals on the circuit. I can't explain how I knew this, other than to say about half of the dancers were breast-enhanced, and the others weren't. Obviously, the road girls had the fake tits and the locals what God have given them. Most of the customers hooted and hollered and even invested in table dances, when the girls had big enough fake tits.

I had zero interest in fake tits, but to each his own. The girl I did find of interest, which is to say who hardened my dick, was clearly local — she was very pretty, blue-eyed, pouty of mouth, with straight blonde, seemingly natural hair, modified by a Farrah Fawcett flip that was a decade or so out of date. She had a pert dimpled ass that defied gravity, and wonderful pale creamy flesh, but her boobs were too small for the room.

They were just right for me. They perched on her rib cage with tip-tilting authority, perfect handfuls that these other cretins couldn't appreciate. This cretin and his throbbing dick were most appreciative. I was on my third beer, by the way.

And in fact, I had just gotten rid of it or anyway its predecessors and was heading back from the john for my table when I felt a hand on my arm, and turned to look right into the little stripper's big blue eyes.

"Can you do me a favor?"

She was either actually asking for a favor, or damn good. No, I didn't think she was in love with me. . . .

"See that guy over there — stuffing a dollar into Heather's g-string? Be subtle."

I flicked a glance at a beefy, make that fat,

biker with a leather cap and more facial hair than two Grateful Dead band members — kind of an awful hair color, too, a yellow that tried to be red but didn't make it.

"He'll want a table dance," she said. "I have to work the room or get fired, so I can't, you know, turn him down or just disappear."

"You want me to buy a table dance, I'll buy a table dance."

This was not nearly as hard as she was making it. Not that she wasn't making it hard. . . .

"He's been here before," she said. "He's persistent. He puts his hand down in my front. I don't do that. I'm not that kind of dancer."

This was interesting to hear, since the Lucky Devil's strip club was raunchy indeed — the girls took off their pasties and g-strings at the end of their first song. And they danced to three songs. . . .

"How can I help?"

"We have a V.I.P. room. We can go in there and stay for a while, and maybe he'll go away or settle for somebody else or something."

"I do want to help, but what's the V.I.P. room cost?"

"I'm not going to charge you anything!

You're helping me."

So I helped her.

She took me into the back room, which was a bunch of easy chairs in open cubicles. No fucking was going on or anything overt; this was not about blow jobs or even hand jobs. This was good, clean, all-American fun, like the so-called dry humps healthy teens used to have under the bleachers at ball games. And I presume they still do, if they have a lick of sense.

The girls kept their pasties on and their g-strings, in the V.I.P. room, but otherwise were naked, and danced for a guy for a song (ten bucks for one, I gathered, twenty-five for three), most of it grinding in his lap or shoving her fake titties in his face and rubbing and rubbing and rubbing some more.

My little blonde did rub her cupcakes in my face a couple times, but mostly she just danced, or straddled my lap and didn't really grind. We just talked. Here's some of it, shouted over loud piped-in music:

"What's your name?"

"Candy."

Bow Wow Wow was doing "I Want Candy." I swear.

"Stage name?"

"Real. Candace."

"You go to school, Candace?"

"I wish. I wanna go to beauty college, but it's expensive."

"You local or on the road?"

"Local. Can't travel. I got a kid."

"Really?"

"Uh huh. Little boy."

"What's his name?"

"Sam. He's five. He goes to kindergarten next year."

"His daddy looking after him?"

"He doesn't have one. A girl who works days, at the grain elevator? She sits with Sam till she goes to work."

"You don't look old enough to have a five-year-old."

"I was fifteen."

"Makes you twenty?"

"I'm twenty. You're nice."

"You're nice, too, Candace."

There was quite a bit more, but that's as interesting as it got, and anyway you get the drift.

She smelled good — most of the dancers were doused in what used to be called dimestore perfume, but she had on Giorgio, or a reasonable facsimile. She had the usual heavy makeup, clownish cheeks, blue eye-shadow, pink lip gloss, but that was par for the course these days even for non-stripper girls. Even though she didn't grind, I had a raging hard-on. My shorts were in ruins.

Another stripper, a skinny brunette with big but real breasts, came over and whispered in Candace's ear, then went away.

Candace beamed at me. "Lover boy's picked somebody else out! He's on his second table dance already. I think I'm in the clear. You're very sweet, Jack."

I had told her my name was Jack.

Then she gave me a kiss.

Long and kind of real.

After that, she gave me a more legit V.I.P. room treatment for the rest of the song ("Hit Me with Your Best Shot"), and then led me back into the strip club. I tried to give her a twenty but I swear (unbelievable, but it happened) she wouldn't take it.

I probably could have bought a legit table dance from her at that point, but I'd had all I could take. I went and sat in the rear of the smoky, mirrored room, focused on fake tits and disco lights until my erection went down, then wandered back into the middle bar. No more beer for me. I asked for and got a Diet Coke.

It was almost one, and I had a game to play.

SEVEN

About the same square footage as the strip club's V.I.P. lounge, the private poker room was tucked behind the Lucky Devil's main bar, though with no access from there. And of course the way in from the casino was guarded by one of those ubiquitous bouncers on boxes.

You've heard of wall-to-wall carpeting — well, this room had carpeting *on* the walls, plush, cream-color stuff, much thicker than the more normal-pile (but same color) carpet on the floor. Matching built-in couches ran along all the walls except the one adjacent the parking lot, which had an exit-only door and, more prominently, a big black padded Naugahyde wet bar with black shelving heavy with booze on one side and a stereo set-up on the other. A busty little platinum blonde in the standard Lucky Devil black spandex minidress was tending bar (and the stereo); right now she was filling bowls with chips and pretzels and such, her big brown eyes having no more expression than her raccoon mascara.

The decor was less eccentric than practical — soundproofing was the order of the day, or night anyway, and the low-slung ceiling tile was part of how this chamber could be so quiet in the thick of a club where each room was noisier than the last. The track lighting was subdued, but the big hexagonal table was the target of a Tiffany-style hanging lamp. Though the billiard felt was new, the table appeared old, its maple handrails showing wear, and the chip wells and drink-holders (despite fresh cork) had the look of a craftsman who'd operated long ago.

I was the first player to arrive, other than my host, a tall, slender guy in a lightweight white suit over a gray shirt and skinny white tie, very hip and New Wave, only his well-oiled Frankie-Avalon-circa-1958 pompadour undercut it. His hands were free of rings, but that was because he'd removed them before starting to shuffle, putting them in his drink well — gold rings encrusted with just a few fewer precious gems than the Maltese Falcon.

Jerry Giovanni, suspiciously tan for a Midwesterner — Florida trips, maybe, or tanning bed access — was almost handsome, a slightly horsier-looking John Travolta.

Pausing in his shuffling, holding the deck in his left hand, he got to his feet, extended a palm and said, "Jerry Giovanni. My friends call me Jerry G."

I shook the hand. Firm. "Jack Gibson, Mr. Giovanni."

He sat, smiled wide, the whiteness of his teeth against the tanned flesh just as startling as the similar effect Richard Cornell achieved, and gestured to the seat opposite him.

"We only have five players tonight, Jack. And call me Jerry G."

"Okay, Jerry G."

"So I was pleased to hear you were joining us. I asked Mandy to have you come in a little early."

"Mandy?"

"Little blackjack dealer. Redhead. She likes you, Jack. I could fix you up. Kid can suck the chrome off a '71 Caddy."

"No, that's okay. I can make friends on my own."

He laughed with a snort, liking that, or pretending to. His eyes were too large for his face and a little close together; guess I already said he had a horsey look. But his snorting laughter emphasized it.

"No offense meant," Jerry G said. "Good-looking fella like you, I'm sure you get more tail than Sinatra."

"Maybe Sinatra *now.*"

He shuffled, did some show-off stuff doing the accordion bit with the deck. Not that smart a move from a guy doing all the dealing.

"You know the house rules, don't you?"

"The house usually does."

He snort-laughed again. "No, no, Jack, I mean, the rules *of* the house. Of this room. It's a thousand-dollar buy in. We don't play table stakes — you can go to your pocket any time. Checks are fine, even items like watches or jewelry, if the players are agreed as to value. But no IOU's."

"Cool."

"I'm the banker, and I'm the dealer. And I play."

"I heard about that. I can live with it. *What* do we play?"

He grinned nice and wide, yards of white teeth and miles of tan skin — this must have been the last thing Custer saw. "Dealer's choice."

I had to laugh. No snorting, though. "I wouldn't mind having that defined a little better."

"Obviously, no wild cards. I'll choose

138

between draw, five-card stud, seven-card stud, and Texas Hold 'Em. I like to mix it up."

"Okay. I appreciate you taking the time to bring me up to speed like this."

The smile settled down and the eyes seemed shrewd suddenly. "No problem, Jack. But that's not why I wanted a few minutes with you."

"All right. Why do you?"

He shuffled, but his eyes watched mine, not the cards. "You're a stranger in town."

What was this, Tombstone?

I said, "I would imagine a lot of 'strangers' come to Haydee's Port."

"But why did you?"

I didn't answer right away.

He jumped on the silence. "One thing, Jack, a lot of people have tried to pull something on me, and on my papa. You know who my papa is?"

I nodded.

He paused in his shuffling to jerk a thumb upward, as if it were God he were referring to and not an old Mafioso. "Different kinds of cops have come here, do-gooders of various varieties, and it's just never worked out for them."

"I came to play poker."

"You understand, we can play kind of

rough, and I don't just mean the cards. This isn't a matter of me asking you if you're a cop, and you saying yes or no or whatever, and we cover the entrapment ground. No. That river out there, it doesn't discriminate between local or federal or reporter or just about anybody who tries to play us."

I never really intended to pretend to be a salesman of vet supplies, at least not for longer than enough to get in the game, and then come clean later. But I could tell I needed to skip a step.

"My name isn't really Jack Gibson," I said.

"What is it then?"

"I haven't told anybody that in a long time. I've used a bunch of names, and I'm using one right now, not Gibson, where I live. And I prefer to keep that private."

"All right. I can understand that. What brings you to Haydee's Port? To the Lucky Devil?"

"I used to do work for the Giardellis. I did quite a few jobs for them, usually through a middleman. I did one directly for Lou Giardelli, not long before he passed."

He had stopped shuffling. He was studying me, eyes tight now, forehead creased, not exactly a frown. Not exactly.

"I came hoping to have a word with your father," I said.

"About what?"

"Rather not say."

"If it concerns my father, it concerns me."

And that was when the first two of our fellow players arrived, and then another showed, and another, and soon we were playing cards.

I have to give Jerry G credit — our interrupted conversation did not seem to throw him off his game. He had good concentration, and played smart cards, marred by an occasional reckless streak. He was friendly to me, often joking between hands, as did they all, but the table talk during play was limited to say the least.

You don't need to be too concerned about the other men at the table. One was a doctor from River Bluff, a surgeon, and another was a lawyer from Fort Madison; both were in their prosperous mid-fifties. Another was a guy from Port City, Iowa, a good sixty miles upriver, who had blue-collar roots and ran a construction business; he was in his late thirties. The player who'd come the farthest was an executive with John Deere who'd come from Moline.

Everybody seemed to know each other, though this did not seem to be a regular group — my take was that a pool of maybe twelve provided the players for these mid-week games.

Jerry G ran the bank out of a small tin box, and we played white chips at fifty, red chips at one hundred, and blue chips at five hundred. You could only bet five hundred on the last round of betting. I admit I was not used to stakes like this, but you soon learn to just play the cards and bet the chips at their relative value. I played conservatively, and did not bluff. If I bet them, I held them.

The players picked up on this early, and started kidding me about it. Before long they had accepted that I simply did not bluff.

With this approach, I was just barely holding my own. I had trouble in particular with Texas Hold 'Em, which was not a game I'd ever played before. Apparently it was a Vegas favorite, and I did my best. I was strongest on draw poker, which is what I'd grown up playing, though the stud hands were the ones that allowed me to build my "never bluffs" reputation.

The game was pleasant — nobody bitched, nobody got mad, nobody was insulting. These were professional men, and even the construction guy had the right tone, and a good sense of humor — he enjoyed saying "fuck" and "shit" in front of these men who never uttered the words unless a really bad loss came their way. Only the surgeon and the construction guy were smokers, and ceiling fans keep the air breathable.

The little barmaid kept the drinks coming, and here I noticed one of Jerry G's little tricks — he was not drinking. I had to watch the barmaid out of the corner of an eye to see that Jerry G's tumblers were being filled not with Scotch but with tea from an under-the-counter pitcher — the boss was like his B girls out front, only pretending to get tipsy. At least he wasn't talking patrons into buying him Dewar's that was really Lipton's.

The music was strictly Vegas — the barmaid was using the turntable, not the CD player, and spinning Frank, Sammy, Dino, Bobby Darin, Keely Smith, Steve Lawrence, that kind of thing. I could see Jerry G, with his heritage, being a traditionalist, but guessed (with that skinny tie of his) that our host might really have preferred Robert Palmer or Kenny Loggins, or in his darker moments maybe Black Sabbath. Most of his guests, however, were of an age that the Vegas lounge lizards were more their style than Ozzy Osbourne biting the head off a bat.

We were set to take a bathroom break around three-thirty, and were playing one last hand before then. Jerry G was dealing a round of Chicago, seven-card stud with the high spade in the hole taking half the pot. There had been some grumbles at the table, since the high spade thing struck several players as damn near offensive as wild cards; but it was clear Jerry G liked to deal a hand of this now and then, so we were all stuck.

The first card dealt me down was the ace of spades. That gave me half the pot, even if the rest of my hand had been warm spit; but it wasn't — by the time the last bet came around, I had a pair of deuces up, plus the ace of hearts, and a piece of shit. But the three cards in my hand included that ace of spades, the ace of diamonds, and another deuce.

I had been betting modestly, getting everybody to stay in. You might almost call that bluffing, or reverse bluffing, anyway. Everybody but the lawyer took the ride — the pot was huge, two grand and change already. I could tell the surgeon probably had either the king or queen or maybe jack of spades down, and he seemed to have a spade flush going. Between me and Jerry G, in betting order, came the contractor, who could have had a jack-high full house going, and if he had the jack of spades as one of his hole cards, he would have to stay in, with a pot like that.

But the bidding had been hot and heavy enough to give him pause. The contractor bet a modest white chip — fifty bucks.

I had half this pot in the bag, and almost certainly the rest of it. I would like to have raised. I would like to have raised maybe one hundred thousand dollars.

But I checked.

The surgeon was next in line, and he raised a blue chip — five hundred clams.

Jerry G, who had two queens up (and might have had the queen of spades down), saw that bet. The contractor said, "Fuck this shit," and folded.

I raised another blue chip.

Everybody gave me looks to kill, since checking and then raising was bad manners, if kosher. But the surgeon took the final raise of another blue chip, which both Jerry G and I saw.

I'd been right on every assumption — the surgeon had the king of spades down and a flush. Jerry G had a queens-high full house and the queen of spades down.

But, like I said, I had the ace of spades in the hole, and an ace-high full house, so I hauled in the chips. Math was never my strong suit, though I had to be four grand ahead on just that round.

The players swore at me good-naturedly, and Jerry G nodded for me to follow him out the exit door.

I was near a little light over the door to the poker room, but he was in the shadows, an arrangement he'd contrived. He offered me a cigarillo, I declined, and he lighted up the little cigar, and regarded the rear expanse of the Giovanni kingdom. At three-thirty A.M. on a Wednesday, the graveled lot was damn near full. A big-hair hooker in a pink spandex minidress was leading a biker like a lamb to the slaughter (or maybe to the slattern) toward one of the eight little trailers that lined the lot at right and left.

"What do you want to talk to my father about, Jack?"

"I mean no offense not telling you, Jerry G. I don't mind if you accompany me. But I need to talk to him in person."

The amber eye of the lighted cigarillo stared at me. "What about, Jack?"

I had a feeling I better take a shot. I took it. "I used to work through a middleman, not directly for your friends in Chicago. There was always insulation. You know about insulation."

"I know about insulation."

146

"So maybe you can figure out what kind of work I used to do."

The cigarillo looked at me; somewhere behind it, Jerry G was looking at me, too. "You don't have the size for a strongarm. You're no pipsqueak, but I wouldn't hire you on as a bouncer, that's for fucking sure."

"I'd get a nosebleed up on those boxes. No, my specialty wasn't handling problems or convincing people not to be problems."

"Your business is *removing* problems."

"Used to be." I held my hands up in surrender, my empty hands. "I retired. I made a lot of money, and I retired."

"So you just happened to be in Haydee's Port."

"I heard a good time could be had."

"Got that right. So, then . . . you just want to pay my papa your respects? I don't think so."

I shook my head. "No. I want to tell him about somebody I saw over at the Paddlewheel. Somebody I recognized."

He settled a hand on my shoulder. Gently. His smile emerged from the darkness, Cheshire Cat style. "Jack, you're going to have to tell me. The only path to my pop is through me. I'm the gatekeeper, *capeesh?*"

I *capeeshed.*

"I saw a guy I'd worked with once in the

147

old days," I said. "He was a specialist in hit-and-run. You know, 'accidents'?"

The hand came off my shoulder, the smile disappeared, and the cigarillo tip stared.

"I believed he was casing that guy Cornell, who runs the Paddlewheel —"

"I know who Cornell is."

"And I think Cornell was his mark."

"*How* do you know, Jack? Did you talk to this old pal of yours?"

Improvising like a jazz soloist, I said, "I only worked one job with him, a long time ago, and that was before I had my face worked on."

"You had a plastic surgery job? That good, was it?"

"My mother wouldn't know me. Anyway, I didn't want any part of it. No skin off my ass if my old 'pal,' as you put it, takes Cornell out. My experience is, anybody with a target on his back probably mostly put it there himself. Fuck the guy."

"All right," Jerry G said.

He'd liked the sound of that, I thought.

"Anyway, last night, or I guess this morning, I was in my car in the Paddlewheel parking lot. I drank too much and fell asleep in the back seat. Something woke me, and I realized it was daylight, and I saw a couple of Cornell's security guys grabbing Monahan. That's his name, Monahan, the hit-and-run specialist."

"What do you mean, grab?"

"Well, more than grab. One of 'em smashed his head into the steering wheel. Then another shoved him over, and took off out of there, and the other Cornell security guy followed in a second car."

"Disposing of the body . . ."

"Obviously."

Silence.

He dropped the cigarillo, crushed it under his heel, and stepped into the light. "And what does this have to do with my father? And me?"

I shrugged. "I didn't just fall off the turnip truck. I can see who around Haydee's Port would want rid of Cornell. If a hit on that guy has gone tits up, I figure you guys would want to know about it."

"Just out of the goodness of your heart."

"Not really. I thought your papa might think the information was worth a buck. Or maybe . . . well, I should save this for him."

He thumped my chest with a finger. Lightly but the threat was there. "No, Jack. Give it to me."

I shrugged. "I thought you might need somebody else to step in, and take care of Cornell."

". . . But you're *retired,* Jack."

I grinned at him. "Yeah, but I retired early. I'm still healthy enough to pick money up in the street."

His tan puss split into a white grin. He and Cornell were two fucking peas in one fucking pod.

He slipped an arm around my shoulder and said, "Let's play cards."

We played cards. I continued to play conservatively, hanging onto my stacks of chips, which were the envy of the others. I continued not to bluff. When my wristwatch said it was nearing six, I finally asked how late we were going to go.

I could see from the expressions around me that the others would have gone on till either hell froze over or they'd won their money back. Neither seemed likely, and our host knew it.

"Once more," he said.

He dealt a simple game of five card stud. I'll cut to the finish, which may be of interest. I had an ace of diamonds up and otherwise bupkus. Jerry had two kings up. We each had two cards down, Jerry having dealt the first and last cards that way. The others had dropped out, and along the way, not a single other ace had been on the board.

Time to bluff.

I had the bet, and tossed out a blue chip.

Jerry G gave me the snort laugh. "You want me to think you've got an ace down, Jack? I don't think you do."

He raised me a blue chip.

So I raised him another blue chip. "It's only five hundred to find out."

He was frowning. I didn't think it was unfriendly, just a deep, thoughtful frown. He was losing. Down maybe three grand.

"Fucker doesn't bluff, Jerry G," the surgeon said.

Jerry G snorted another laugh and threw in his cards. Because it was the last round, though, he gathered all the cards, and I noted him discreetly checking my hand, to see what I'd had. He flinched, but resisted the urge to let everybody know I had indeed, finally, been bluffing. He hadn't bought the right to see those cards, after all, and that was bad manners indeed.

Jerry G cashed everybody in. I was up six thousand and change above the five thousand I'd brought along. Hands were shaken all around, the little barmaid provided everybody with coffee and sweet rolls (the coffee in Styrofoam to-go cups to prevent the group from lingering), and soon Jerry G and I were by ourselves.

"Let's talk outside," he said.

I followed him, and two guys grabbed me. One was the big bald black bastard and the other was the limp-nose prick from the dance club. They dragged me out of the lot and into an alleyway between the Lucky Devil and some other dive, and Jerry G followed along. I have no idea how he set it up, other than maybe enlisting his goons by way of a whispered command he'd given the barmaid. He'd risen from the table to do this more than once, and she'd slipped out several times, presumably for supplies, and now I was up against a brick wall, the black guy holding onto my one arm, the noseless guy onto the other, doing my Jesus on the cross impression.

"You're working for Cornell," Jerry G said, grinning at me, and it was a vicious thing, a horsey look worthy of a stallion getting ready to kick your head in. "You were seen there, you were heard there, and I gave you a chance to play it straight, but you thought you'd fuck me, didn't you?"

"I did talk to Cornell! I hadn't finished telling you —"

"No, you *are* finished."

And Jerry G walked away, into the dawning day, while in the darkness, the two bouncers took turns. I felt a fist rattle my teeth, and another bash my nose, then my belly played punching bag first for one, then the other, while I coughed and gurgled on blood. I wish I could tell you this is where I came roaring back, but the truth is, I fell to my knees and then my face found the filthy brick floor of the alley and I got used to the taste of blood while they kicked me in the ass and the ribs, and finally the toe of a shoe caught the side of my head.

My last thought was, *Shouldn't have bluffed the fucker. . . .*

EIGHT

Somebody was asking me a question.

A woman. A girl. *Some* kind of female. . . .

I couldn't make it out, but I felt hands on me, small, struggling to get hold of me, trying to lift me, but I just wanted to sleep.

"Come on . . . *come on* . . . get to your feet. They might come *back. . . .*"

As those words came into aural focus, so did the pain, starting with a blinding headache. I opened my eyes, saw a blur, and shut them again. I was on my side, on something hard, but moving only made it worse. My instinct was to stay put.

"Get *up. . . .*"

The hands pulled on me, and I found myself standing, through no real effort of my own, a broken puppet whose improbable limbs went in every direction but the right ones, operated by an unseen puppeteer, and the headache eased just a little to let in the pools of pain that were throbbing in seemingly random regions around what had once been my body.

"You have to *help*. . . . They're coming *back*. . . ."

That was when I remembered where I was, if not who I was, and what had happened before I took my nap on a brick bed, specifically that I'd been beaten bloody, and not long ago, because the blood was still warm and wet in my mouth and on my face.

I willed my feet to support me and my legs went along with it and my eyes focused enough to tell my savior was the little blonde stripper I'd done the favor for. She was in a black silk baseball-type jacket and her makeup was off and her hair was ponytailed back and she looked about twelve. She also looked scared shitless.

"You have a car?" she asked.

What the fuck was this, small talk?

But I nodded.

"Parked close?"

She was on my right, helping my legs hold me up. With my left hand, my wrist limper than Paul Lynde's, I gestured toward the street.

"Ponty," I said.

She was walking down the alley toward daylight and the street. "Pontiac?"

"Boo," I said. Not trying to scare her: trying to say . . .

"Blue?"

She paused at the mouth of the alley where daylight blinded me. A few moments, and I could see, sort of. Nobody on the street. Not a car moving. Not a pedestrian. I willed my neck to turn two inches to the right and said, "There. . . ."

"Two-tone blue?"

"Yeah."

We were close to it. She only had to drunk-walk me twenty feet before leaning me against the side of the Sunbird. She looked all around her, like a frightened bird, while one of her little hands dug in my front pants pocket, digging, searching. Not as much fun as it sounds.

I heard the jangle of the car keys as she drew them out and she unlocked the door on the rider's side, and stuffed me in, shut me in, and came around and got in on the driver's side.

"I don't take my car to work," she said.

I had no comment.

The Sunbird was moving.

"I'm only a few blocks away. Usually walk it. But I can't walk *you* that far."

Interesting information, but again, I let it pass. I was busy waiting to see if my head would come apart in pieces like a barrel

156

with the rungs removed.

"Stay awake," she said. "Stay awake till we get there."

The unpaved side street she pulled onto made for a rough ride. I understood how a pinball machine must have felt when a ball was running around loose inside it and smacking into things. But it kept me awake.

She pulled up at a mobile home, yellow and white, not very big. A red Mustang circa 1969 was parked out at the curb, where rust was eating it. No sidewalk, no trees. A row of mobile homes, maybe six, but who was counting?

"Candy," I said. I was not requesting food.

She was struggling to get me pried out of the rider's side and onto my feet. "What?"

"Your name."

"You don't miss much, do you, Jack?"

She remembered my name, too.

She was walking me past the Mustang onto and across a tiny front yard where crab grass was trying to grow and failing. Like a bad hair transplant.

The hardest part was her getting me up the three wooden steps, and not having me fall back down them while she held onto me with one hand and tried to unlock the door with the other. She couldn't quite get the key in the slot and finally just pounded a tiny fist on the wood and yelled, "*Honey? Are you up?*"

She waited, and then the door opened. A little kid, maybe three-and-half feet tall, blond, blue-eyed, blank, in *Star Wars* pajamas, opened it. He didn't seem surprised to see his mother lugging a strange man with blood on him. It was that kind of town.

The kid didn't pitch in after that, except to shut the door behind us. He returned to the floor in front of the little TV on a stand where he was eating a Pop Tart and *Sesame Street* puppets were doing a better job of staying upright than I was.

The trick after that was her navigating me around and through an elaborate wooden train track that took up a lot of the midget living room's threadbare green carpet.

She moved me down a little hallway, sideways because there wasn't room for two abreast, and then guided me into a small bedroom, putting me on my back on top of a sunflower bedspread.

I passed out.

Some minutes later, I woke up and was wearing nothing except my jockey shorts. The bruises weren't showing much yet, but she was checking me over, and had a little bowl of warm water and a washcloth she was using to clean the blood off my face.

"I don't think you have any broken bones," she said.

"Ribs are sore."

"Could have a broken rib. There's an emergency room in River Bluff, if that's what you want."

I shook my head, which was a mistake.

"Shit," I said, as the blinding headache knifed across the back of my eyes.

"Your nose isn't broken," she said.

"Should be."

She wasn't in the baseball jacket now. She had on a B-52's t-shirt and denim cut-offs. Did I say she looked about twelve? Without her makeup.

"You got any aspirin?" I asked. My lips felt thick. My tongue felt thicker.

"No. Better."

She got up and I admired her ass as she receded down the hall. This did not mean I was feeling better. Lenny Bruce told a joke about a guy in car accident who lost a foot and made a pass at the nurse in the ambulance. Difference between men and women.

I took the two pills she brought me and swallowed some water. "What was that?"

"Percodan."

". . . Thank you."

I passed out, or went to sleep.

Take your pick.

■ ■ ■ ■

When I woke up, I realized the little bedroom had blackout curtains. I felt stiff, and I felt sore, and I had a dull headache, but not throbbing. I wondered how many hours I'd been out. Sunlight was peeking in around the edge of the dark curtains, so it couldn't have been too very long.

She heard me stirring, and came in to check on me. She had a different t-shirt on, a pink Cyndi Lauper one, but the denim cut-offs looked familiar.

I asked her, "What time is it?"

"It's about ten."

Ten A.M., huh? I was a resilient motherfucker — a couple hours sleep, and good as new. Not bad for thirty-five.

"Friday," she added.

"No. This is . . . Thursday, right?"

"No. You slept round the clock. Except for twice when I woke you up, led you to the bathroom, then fed you Percodan."

"Fuck. No wonder I feel like somebody emptied me out and filled me with molasses. I don't remember you doing that at all."

"You weren't very talkative." She perched on the edge of the bed. "You look better. You don't have a black eye or anything."

I flipped the covers back. The deep blue bruising crawled in amoeba-like blotches over half a dozen places. I was breathing deep and the ribs weren't hurting, though. Small miracle I hadn't busted one. That is, had one busted for me.

I covered and sat up, which didn't hurt any more than falling down a flight of stairs. She propped an extra pillow behind me.

"Hungry?" she asked.

"I could try to eat."

"There's left-over alphabet soup from Sam's lunch."

"Sam's your kid?"

"Sam's my kid."

"Alphabet soup please."

"Grilled cheese sandwich, maybe? Milk?"

I was a kid home sick from school.

"Grilled cheese, perfect. You wouldn't have any kind of Coke, would you?"

"Diet Pepsi."

I wasn't going to insult my hostess. "That would be swell."

She sat and watched me eat off a tray in bed and I began to feel vaguely human. The little boy came in, wearing a red t-shirt and blue shorts, and tugged on his mother's arm and whispered something, and she went off and tended to *that* kid for a while.

When she came back, I was done eating,

161

and I found a place for the tray on the little nightstand. "Why are you doing this? Why did you help me last night? I mean . . . night before last?"

"You helped me."

"Candace," I said, trying to impress her by not shortening her name to the more stripper-like Candy, "all I did was let you give me a free table dance. I have a feeling a lot of Good Samaritans would have done that."

"You didn't take advantage. You were nice. I'm a good judge of character."

No, she wasn't.

"Anyway, I've seen how people just disappear around the Lucky. And I didn't want that to happen to you."

"Those two bouncers who jumped me . . . do I remember you saying they were heading back for me?"

She nodded. "I've seen them do that before. They take somebody in the alley, work them over. Then they pull a car over and throw the poor person in the back seat or trunk, and drive off."

That didn't mean Jerry G had intended having me killed, just that they were going to dump me off the premises. A ditch somewhere, or a parking lot across the river. Or, they could have killed my ass, and tossed me in the river. Either way, Candace was a rare angel in Haydee's.

"Why do you work there, Candace? You're a pretty, intelligent girl. You could do better."

She smiled and laughed. "I'm pretty, but I'm not that smart. I never got better than C's, and I dropped out my sophomore year. I have a little boy to support, who the H knows where his father is, and I hope to do better for myself, so for right now? Nothing pays better than dancing at the Lucky. Not for me."

I didn't want to insult her, but I had to ask. I tried as delicately as possible: "That's all you do at the Lucky? Dance?"

She didn't take offense. "I'm not one of Jerry G's party girls. They don't make all that much more than I do, anyway, by the time Jerry gets his slice, and they risk a lot. Some of their customers can get rough."

"Rougher than your biker pal?"

"Way rougher. That's real sad, those girls. Jerry G gets 'em all hooked. Free drugs at first, then so much of their pay goes to it, they just sort of spin their wheels. I don't take drugs. I don't even smoke grass, anymore. Not around Sam, anyway."

Good-naturedly, I reminded her, "You have Percodan around."

"I work long hours, on my feet, shaking my bottom, always around a lot of smoke, and sometimes I get bad headaches. I can buy those pills at work, but I'm careful. You can get addicted to that shit, y'know."

"I don't smoke or drink much or do drugs," I said. "I'm the clean-cut guy you've been dreaming about, Candace."

She grinned; her gums showed a little, as her teeth were rather tiny — it was endearing. "What are you, a priest?"

"I didn't say I was celibate."

"I didn't think you were." Still grinning. "I was sitting on your lap the other night, remember?"

"I remember. . . . I hope I don't get you in any trouble. I'm sure your boss wouldn't be thrilled with you, if he knew you'd bailed me out."

She shook her head; the ponytail flounced. "Nobody saw me. We're fine. We'll just get you healed up and healthy, and you can find some other town to have fun in."

I didn't argue the point.

We chatted for a while, and she told me her long-term plans, which were to save enough money to sell the trailer, move to Des Moines where her older sister lived, and go to beauty school. She wanted to buy a nicer car, too. She had about ten thousand saved, and another fifteen thousand or so would make her dreams come true.

Which reminded me.

I'd had eleven thousand in cash on me. Surely part of the point of that roust in the alley had been to retrieve Jerry G's poker losses; but I didn't remember that happening. Not that I would, busy as I was getting the shit kicked out of me and bleeding out my nose and mouth.

"Could you bring me my pants?" I asked.

"You're not getting *up* already?"

"No, I just want to check something."

She jerked a thumb. "Well, I'm washing them, your shirt and pants. They were pretty filthy from that alley. But there was some stuff in the pockets."

After disappearing briefly, she came in with my wallet and a thick fold of bills.

"You must have won," she said, eyes big.

I counted it. Nothing was missing from the wallet, including the phony credit cards I was using.

Christ, they'd half-killed me, and left all that dough on me? Maybe they intended to clean me when they returned to take me for a ride. Or maybe the beating hadn't been about the poker game at all. Maybe Jerry G's pride in his own poker playing was too high to allow him to help himself to another player's rightful winnings, even when he was planning to have that player beaten like a red-headed stepchild.

"What kind of boss is Jerry G?" I asked her.

She was perched on the edge of the bed again. "If you don't cross him, he's no problem. He doesn't take a cut of my tips. If I sit and talk to a client, and get him to buy me a drink, that's split between the house and the girl."

"What does he pay you to dance?"

"Nothing."

"You shitting me?"

"No. It's strictly the dollars in our g's, and the table dances and V.I.P. lounge tips. And we don't date the customers. Jerry G says, if we want to do it for money, he'll get us a little trailer out back."

"What about Gigi?"

"Jerry G's pop? He's a nice enough old guy. He used to be a horndog, I hear — they say he used to audition all the girls who were tricking. But he's been sick, lately."

"How sick?"

"Well, I don't know. But he goes to the doctor once a month. Otherwise, he hardly comes down from his suite. He sometimes has breakfast with Jerry G, at that little café downtown."

"Not at the Wheelhouse restaurant?"

"No! Jerry G stays away from the Paddle-wheel and the Wheelhouse. There's a real rivalry there. The girls say Jerry G hates that guy, Cornell. Richard Cornell?"

"Ever been to the Paddlewheel?"

"No. That's one world. The Lucky is another."

"Pretty rough world, for a sweet kid like you."

Her smile was a chin-crinkler. "Are you flirting?"

"Not yet. I just mean, prostitution, gambling, narcotics. . . ."

"Those kinds of things have been around forever. Didn't you ever hear of Sodom and Gomorrah?"

"Sodom, anyway. Doesn't bother you?"

"I'm responsible only to myself, Jack. I have a nice body, and I don't think being naked is sinful or evil or anything. If it makes men happy to see me dance, to feel my boobies in their face or put their hands on my bottom, that's okay by me . . . long as they pay the freight. I have a kid to provide for. I don't trick, and I don't let anybody touch me in my private place."

"Nobody ever?"

"Now you *are* flirting."

"Maybe a little."

She sighed, looked at her hands, which were folded in her lap. Her nails were painted hot pink. "Look, I know the Lucky is a rough place. It's like . . . everybody has to put their time in, in some hellhole in this life. It's an awful, corrupt place, and Jerry G is like the little Godfather of the place."

"Running downtown Haydee's Port isn't that big a deal in the scheme of things, is it?"

"Oh, it's more than just the Lucky Devil — like, Jerry G runs all *kinds* of narcotics up and down the river. They have boats that look like, you know, summer outing kind of stuff. But you'd be shocked at how much of that . . . *evil* stuff moves through this tiny little town, and all across the country."

"Were you raised a churchgoer, by any chance, Candace?"

"I went to a Baptist church when I was at home. I haven't been in years. I don't like church, really. But I believe in Jesus. Do unto others and all that stuff."

"You *must,* hauling my ass out of that alley. . . . You got any more of that Percodan?"

"I'll get you another dose. But be careful — you don't want to get hooked."

I took the Percodan and went back to sleep for a while. When I woke up, the clock on the nightstand said one, and sunlight was still edging in around the dark curtains, so I didn't figure I'd slept another day away or anything.

What was interesting was the presence of Candace next to me, under the sheets. Shouldn't have surprised me, since this was her bed, after all, and she worked nights, and had to catch some rest some time.

She was sound asleep, even snoring a little, and wearing another t-shirt and sheer panties. She was nestled against me, with her head on my chest, my arm around her, her slender arm draped across my side.

I was just staring at her, wondering what my life would have been like if a sweet kid like this had married me back in the Nam days, and not a cheating little cunt.

I was also thinking about my close call — without her sweet nature and Baptist up-bringing, I might have been dead right now, dumped in a ditch or maybe in the drink.

Seemed to me I had about come to the end of this way of life. I was lucky I hadn't already been killed, trying to play the Broker's database like a loose slot machine. I was dealing with murderers and their deserving clients, trying to play both ends against the middle, only I was always the guy in the middle, wasn't I?

If I could make that substantial financial

killing in Haydee's Port, I might be able to invest in Wilma's Welcome Inn and start living the kind of life actual human beings experienced. Maybe I could even find a nice kid like Candace, who had now turned her back to me. I risked turning onto my side, and didn't die of a hemorrhage, so I spooned with her. She snuggled her bottom against my groin and a mighty oak grew.

She began giggling, in her sleep maybe, and a hand reached around, and found my dick and stroked it like a puppy, while I purred like a kitten. She turned over and whispered, "Sam's napping, so. . . ." And she gave me the finger-to-the-lips *shush* sign.

Then her right hand slipped in the front of my jockey shorts and withdrew the only part of me that was throbbing in a good way, and her little mouth with the full lips suckled on the tip, then began to slide up and down, her tongue working miracles that had surely not been revealed to her at the Baptist Church.

She had me to the brink, when she stopped and asked, "You want to come this way? Or do you feel good enough to . . . ?"

Keeping faith with her Baptist roots, I got on her Missionary style, but only after she had slipped out of the panties and pulled off the t-shirt. Her pert breasts stayed that way, on her back, and when I slipped inside her, she was so tight, she might have been holding me in her fist.

It lasted a surprisingly long time, and I felt every ache and pain from the other night but somehow it only added to the sensation. She looked up at me with that face free of makeup, looking only twelve but fucking like twenty, her expression begging mercy, understanding and forgiveness. What she got turned her chest and neck and cheeks scarlet and made her nipples point skyward and her eyes the same direction with her mouth making a little O to go with the big one.

Me, I came so hard my soul might have been escaping me, if it hadn't fled long before.

We did that darn near silently, not waking Sam from his nappy-poo, and she took a shower and I took a shower and we both sat, fully dressed now, at a little table off her kitchen nook, feeling vaguely embarrassed, yet knowing we'd made a memory that neither of us would ever lose, at least till she died of natural causes and somebody put a bullet in my head.

Then I asked her about Gigi Giovanni and his doctor appointments. Would she happen to know when his next one was?

"Funny you should ask," she said. "It's always the third Friday of the month."

"What's today, the second Friday?"

"No, silly. The third."

NINE

The River Bluff Neurology Clinic was in Rivercrest Medical Park, a beautifully landscaped collection of recently erected one-story red-brick buildings with interconnecting drives and several shared parking lots — a sort of shopping mall for the sick.

This was West River Bluff, where I'd wound up following a dark-green late model Lincoln Town Car from the Lucky Devil parking lot. Enough vehicles had been there for me not to call attention to myself and, anyway, there was no reason to think any of Jerry G's people would recognize my wheels. I sat parked between a pick-up truck and a Dodge Daytona and watched for almost an hour, thinking I'd probably missed my moment.

The only thing that had given me hope was that Lincoln Town Car, parked near the casino portion of the Lucky Devil. Hanging around near the Lincoln was a big guy with a butch haircut and a black suit with a tie-less white shirt, smoking one cigarette after another, occasionally leaning against the driver door, now and then checking his watch.

Finally Jerry G, in a yellow sport shirt and rust-color slacks, came out a casino exit, helping an older gent toward the car. Jerry G was smiling and talking, one arm around his charge, the other guiding him along. The old boy was short and squat but not really fat, not anymore; his head was squarish and his snow-white hair neatly barbered but indifferently combed. He wore a double-breasted wide-lapel gray pinstripe suit that had been in style a couple of times in the twentieth century, just not at the moment.

Was Jerry G going to accompany his pop to the doctor's appointment? That was who this was — Giorgio "Gigi" Giovanni, and I wasn't guessing, because I had done enough work for that family to have seen all the main players at one time or another, if from a distance.

No — Jerry G was depositing his pop in back of the Town Car, and the butch-hair boy was tossing a smoke to the gravel and coming around to get behind the wheel. They pulled out, Jerry G lingering to watch them go, then he headed back in. The Lincoln had exited the lot — access was strictly in back of the Lucky Devil, on a gravel strip along a row of trees — but catching up was no problem. Besides, I wanted to make sure I always had at least one car between us, and when I fell in behind them on the toll bridge, I had a two-car cushion.

Wearing sunglasses — not a disguise, this was a sunny day — I had followed them through the rolling city to its west outskirts and the medical complex. The Lincoln took a handicapped space, and I pulled around to park as far away as possible, at least for the moment. I watched while the burly chauffeur helped the old man out of the back seat, and walked him up a gently slanting walk to the double doors of the modern clinic.

When they were inside, I moved the car closer — I didn't take a handicapped space, because I may be a killer but I'm not a prick, and anyway I didn't have one of those hanging plastic cards that fend off fines. I wanted to be close in case I needed a quick getaway.

This might seem amusing, particularly since several other elderly patients were being helped into the clinic by relatives or whatever, indicating the facility was primarily geriatric. I would grant you few quick getaways had ever been made from this building.

On the other hand, that chauffeur was a big fucker, and the only reason I was walking around after that beating by his bouncer brothers was the Percodans perking in my bloodstream. Plus, that suitcoat hung loose enough that a handgun might be snugged under his armpit, and I was currently unarmed.

He was driving around the supposed godfather of Haydee's Port, after all, a character with genuine Chicago bona fides — old Gigi only missed getting himself an episode of *The Untouchables* by maybe a decade.

A sign on the brick by the front doors spelled out the specialty of the house — neurology — and I went on into a small waiting room populated by senior citizens and their keepers. Nobody looked very bright-eyed, including the keepers. Two rows of chairs on either side faced each other, divided by a big coffee table where old magazines went to die.

I selected a *Highlights,* read for a while about Goofus and Gallant (speaking of pricks, how about that fucking Goofus?), and after ten minutes the nurse receptionist, a plump woman bursting her whites, called, *"George Giovanni!"*

Giovanni did not react, but the butch-hair bodyguard did, smirking disgustedly as he tossed his *Sports Illustrated* swimsuit issue on the coffee table, to rise and haul the old boy around and down a hallway at left.

I waited, and about ninety seconds later, the bodyguard returned, alone, and retrieved his reading matter.

I got up, went up to the porcine nurse (what the fuck kind of health message was *she* sending?) and asked where the men's room was. I already knew, having spotted it from where I'd been sitting — it was down that same hallway where Giovanni had been walked, and abandoned.

She pointed toward the men's room, mildly irritated (yeah, those bodily functions are a real nuisance), and I went down the hallway. It wasn't a big place, maybe four little examining rooms, and they all had patient charts hanging on the door. The second chart I checked said "George H. Giovanni."

Nobody else was in the hallway, and the fat nurse was busy resenting her lot in life, so I thumbed through the sheets. I'm no doctor, but the word "dementia" jumped out. Among the pages clipped to the board were several tests taken by Mr. Giovanni, including the faces of clocks that had been

177

filled in with floating hands, as if Dali and a four-year-old had collaborated, and several pieces of startling news, including that Nixon was still president and that the patient's favorite color was "ice cream."

I went in, leaving the chart on the door, and said pleasantly to the little old man sitting on the edge of the examining table, "And how are you today, Mr. Giovanni?"

"Who are you?"

"I'm Dr. Leefer." That was the name on the chart, anyway. "How have you doing, Mr. Giovanni? Are the medications helping?"

I'd seen the names of the meds, but they were Greek to me. Right now, from my point of view, anything that wasn't Percodan wasn't pertinent.

"I'm doin' okay, doc."

"And how is your son doing?"

He frowned. The face that had once been fearsome was a lined, sunken thing, like a fruit that had gone off, and the eyes had less alertness than your average chimp. "I have a son?"

"You sure do."

"Well, I'll be damned!"

"His name is Jerry."

"Yes! Jerry! He's a good boy."

"He's taking care of you all right?"

"Yes. Yes. Can't complain."

"Getting what you need to eat and drink?"

"Yes. I get plenty of ice cream. All the ice cream I want."

"That's wonderful. Do you know who I am?"

"Don't you know?"

"I'm the doctor — Dr. Leefer."

"Well, that's right! Dr. Leefer."

"Do you know a man named Cornell?"

"Do I?"

"Richard Cornell. Do you know him?"

"No. Can't say I do. Might. I forget people's names sometimes."

"What about a place called the Paddle-wheel? Do you know that place?"

"No. Is it a boat?"

"No, it's a gambling house."

"The Lucky Devil is a gambling house."

"Right. Your son runs it for you, doesn't he?"

"Yes. My son. Is his name Jerry?"

"Yes it is."

"Who are you again?"

"Your doctor. Dr. Leefer."

"I'm staying on my pills."

"That's good, Mr. Giovanni. That's good." The door opened and we both jumped a little. A guy with a Freud beard and no hair on his head and goggle-size eyeglasses came in, checking his clipboard. He had a name tag that said DR. LEEFER. He frowned at me.

"And *you* are?" he asked.

The old man answered for me: "He's my doctor."

"If he's your doctor, Mr. Giovanni, who am I?"

"Don't you know?" The old boy nodded toward me. "Maybe Dr. Leefer here can tell you."

I stood. Went over to the doc and said, "I'm his nephew Al — Al Giovanni in from Chicago, Dr. Leefer. How's he doing? He seems a little confused."

He frowned at me. "Were you in an accident, Mr. Giovanni?"

He could see the contusions and scrapes on my face.

"No, I had a little altercation across the river. Haydee's Port?"

"Ah," he said, accepting that.

"But I am really am concerned about my uncle. . . ."

He tried not to sigh and almost succeeded. He spoke softly: "Well, I've explained all this to Mr. Giovanni's son. This is not senility, nor do I think we're looking at Alzheimer's. Mr. Giovanni has suffered, and continues to suffer, minor strokes.

They've caused no physical disability to date, but his memory is severely affected. But I'm glad you're here, Mr. Giovanni."

"Are you? Good."

Dark eyebrows rose over the big eyeglass lenses. "Mr. Giovanni's son hasn't accompanied his father to the last *three* appointments, and I need to stay abreast of how Mr. Giovanni is doing at home. He's been able to dress himself, bathe himself, fix himself small meals. Watches television, and can enjoy himself in, shall we say, the moment. Or that *has* been the case — I obviously can't ask Mr. Giovanni about these things himself, which is why it's better if his son would take a stronger interest. I don't mean to be judgmental, but if Mr. Giovanni can no longer perform these simple tasks, he will need a different kind of long-term care."

"To the best of my knowledge," I said, "he's still able to do those things, dress himself and so on."

"Good. That's very good to hear. Now, I'm going to give your uncle a series of cognitive tests. Would you like to sit in?"

"No, no, doc — I think having me here might distract the old fella. You do your thing, and I'll just wait outside . . . So long, Uncle Gigi."

"So long, Dr. Leefer," he said.

I found my way out, the nurse giving me a glare (I'd clearly really exceeded the toilet time limit), moved through the waiting room where the bodyguard was holding his magazine sideways, and went out to my car.

No fast getaway necessary.

After I called from the bar downstairs, Cornell received me in his third-floor office. The Paddlewheel was open — it was around six-thirty — but business wasn't bustling yet, as this was not exactly a place where you went for the early bird special.

He emerged from the bedroom, tying a black rope belt around his maroon dressing gown; his legs were bare and as tanned as George Hamilton's neck and his feet were in slippers. He was lighting up a cigarette and his unblinking aqua-blue eyes narrowed, taking me in.

"What happened to you?" he asked, so concerned he flopped into the nearest overstuffed brown leather chair as he tossed a spent match in an ashtray.

I sat nearby on the matching couch. Cocaine ghosts haunted the glass coffee table.

I said, "Two of Jerry G's greeters took me out back and beat the fuck out of me."

His eyes tightened a little. "You all right?"

Was there an end to his compassion?

"I am, now. This happened Wednesday, or really Thursday morning, and I slept round the clock. Nothing broken. This is what that hazardous duty pay is for."

"Drink?"

I had trained him not to say drinky-poo.

"I could stand a Diet Coke."

He called, *"Chrissy!"*

The bedroom door opened and the little babe with the big yellow perm emerged, painting her nails red. She had on black panties and half a white t-shirt, the underside of pert breasts showing.

"What?"

"Fix me up with a drink, and my friend with a Diet Coke."

She zombie-walked over to the bar, painting her nails all the way, not blessing either of us with a glance. She was efficient, though, and only two minutes or so passed before Cornell had a tumbler of Scotch and ice cubes and I had a cold can of Diet Coke.

"Thanks," I said. "Things go better with Coke, you know."

She said nothing, her lips almost forming a smirk but lacking the enthusiasm for that commitment. She padded into the bedroom, the perfect moons of her bottom exposed below the cut of the panties. She could have used a spanking. So could my dick.

Alone again, my employer and I made a half-hearted toast, and he said, "Why don't you fill me in?"

"I don't do details. I can tell you've I've determined, to my satisfaction anyway, that the old man is out of it."

The tanned forehead formed white creases. "Out of . . . what?"

"It. Any contract on you, any aspect of running the Lucky Devil in particular and downtown Haydee's Port in general, anything greater than putting on his pants, wiping his bottom and warming up some cocoa."

He grinned, a white slash in the tan puss, but his forehead kept on frowning. "What is he, senile?"

"As good as. He's had a bunch of little strokes, and Jerry G is Chief Big Shit now. Sonny Boy apparently hasn't advertised papa's delicate condition because the old reprobate has a big rep, and Jerry still needs to bask in it."

Cornell shook his head. "I hate to say it, but Jerry G has something of a reputation himself. That's one of the reasons why this Chicago conflict, between the Giardelli brothers, continues to just simmer, never

boil over. The status quo is too appealing —
me running the Paddlewheel effectively, and
profitably . . . and Jerry G doing the same
with his sleazeball operation downtown."

"I believe Jerry G does more than just run
the Lucky Devil," I said. "I think some
major drug-running is going on, and Christ
knows what other contraband. We *are* right
on the river."

"I've heard the scuttlebutt." He shrugged,
swirled the liquid in its tumbler, studied it
as if looking for tea leaves to read. "So —
it's just Jerry G, then. Are you prepared to
go forward?"

"With what?"

He frowned. "What the hell do you *think,*
love? Handling the Jerry G problem."

"You want him gone, I'm fine with that.
But I haven't got the goods on him."

The forehead creased again. "What goods
are those?"

"Making sure Jerry G took out the hit.
How do you know this didn't emanate
straight from Chicago?"

He waved that off. "No. No, it's Jerry G.
Has to be."

"Dickie bird, I think he knew I was working for you, when he had me taken out to
the woodshed. He could have had them kill
me, but he didn't. Why?"

185

His shrug was elaborate. "Perhaps Jerry G thought it would backfire on him — he'd get his ass in a wringer with the Chicago family, killing one of my people."

"He'd fear that, but take *you* out? Does that really make sense?"

He smiled on half his face, his expression as patronizing as his tone. "Of course it does. One killing of a subordinate can lead to more such killings, which can lead to a battle here in Haydee's Port that could become an all-out *war* in Chicago."

"Whereas removing you would be the kind of single stroke that could change everything all at once?"

"Right-o. That's how I see it, at least."

I sipped my Diet Coke. Shrugged. "So the job is, take care of Jerry G?"

"Yes. Are we agreed as to price?"

"Considering the work I did eliminating the old man from the equation, let's call it thirty."

He considered that. Then he shrugged. "All right. For all the grief it'll save me, it's a goddamn bloody bargain."

Soon I was downstairs on the main floor, heading past the dining room toward the Paddlewheel exit when a husky female voice called from the bar: "Jack! Come say hello."

In a little black dress that exposed a nice

amount of bosom, redheaded Angela was in her favorite booth, sitting with a yellow pad in front of her, smoking a cigarette as she made notes.

I joined her. "You go on this early?"

"No. This is just the closest thing I have to an office. Going over my set list. Making a few changes." She turned the wide-set green eyes loose on me, and they quickly tightened in concern, as she took in my colorful face. "My God! What happened to *you*?"

"Couple of Jerry G's guys took me through the Jane Fonda workout. Do I look slimmer?"

She touched my hand. "You take awful chances, don't you? I thought . . . nothing."

"What?"

"I hoped to hear from you. I . . . the other day, morning I mean, at your room . . . rather sweet. On the . . . *special* side, I thought."

"A lot more pleasant workout, I'll grant you. Hey, I'm sorry, I really did get my ass handed to me, and I've been recuperating."

She gave me a smirky kiss of a smile. "Then you weren't shacked up with some sweet young thing?"

"Yeah, right. I was cheating on you, screwing a twenty-year-old stripper."

187

That made her laugh. I love telling the truth; often the best way not to be believed. . . .

"You wouldn't want to stop by and catch my last set? Maybe buy me breakfast?"

"I better take a rain check. I'm on the clock."

The green eyes widened. "On the clock, *around* the clock?"

"Right now I am."

Out that hallway, where the private elevator emptied, trotted Cornell's little squeeze, Chrissy, yellow permed curls held by a hot-pink sweatband, making her head look like a ginger ale bottle that fizzed over. She was in tight jeans and a hot-pink shirt tied in a big knot under her pert boobs, and her feet were shod in sandals that showed off red toenails, to match the fingernails she'd been painting. All freshened up, pink lip gloss, blue eye shadow, and no white powder on her nose at all. . . .

"What's the story on baby Madonna?" I asked.

"She's just the latest little lay on Dickie's roster," Angela said, light but with a bitter edge, letting smoke out her nose like a lovely dragon. "One little blow-up doll's pretty much like any other."

"Does she live with him out at the plantation? Or maybe up in his Hefner hideout upstairs?"

"No. She's from River Bluff. Another of these community college girls, if you can believe it."

I didn't, actually.

"Excuse me," I said, and smiled at her, and she gave me a curious look that I let hang.

When I got to the parking lot, Chrissy was pulling out in a red Firebird convertible with a CRYSEE vanity plate — Illinois, not Iowa, where the community college was. I moved toward my lesser Pontiac, but didn't run or anything.

Pretty sure I knew where she was headed.

Ten

At a quarter till eight or so, the Lucky Devil parking lot wasn't close to full. This was a Friday, and one of their big nights, but the Lucky was chiefly an after-hours joint, so Chrissy had no problem finding a parking spot near the building.

I took a space in the row behind her, shut off the engine and sat in the dark watching her, trying to figure out what the fuck to do. Tailing Chrissy's Firebird to the Lucky hadn't allowed a stopover at the Wheelhouse motel to grab my spare nine millimeter.

So I didn't have a gun on me. And I didn't have a plan. All I had was my brute strength, and we've seen how well that had served me in this venue. . . .

Well, maybe I had a *vague* plan.

The Lucky Devil parking lot was about as handy as a pair of gloves with two lefts — the three doors facing the lot all were exit only: that one off the soundproofed private poker room, another off the casino, and one with FIRE EXIT ONLY written on it for the strip club.

To gain entry, you had to cut over to the sidewalk and walk around the building, or cut through the alley where not long ago I'd had so much fun. I figured to watch Chrissy and follow her on whichever path she chose, and intercept her before she could go in, only *fuck me sideways* — she was heading for the casino exit!

And now she was knocking on the thing. . . .

It must have taken a while for the bouncer to climb down off his perch and answer her insistent pounding. He was unfamiliar to me, a bushy-brown-bearded bruiser bursting his black Lucky Devil polo with both muscles and fat, and he was not happy to be disturbed.

Finally emerging from her self-absorbed stupor, Chrissy was animated, words and spittle flying out of her. The bearded guy scowled, nodded, but shut the door on her. She dug into her little pink purse and got out some cigarettes and was lighting up when I grabbed her.

"Let's talk," I said, and the cigarette hit the gravel as I pulled her by the arm toward my car. The night was unseasonably chill, and her nipples were erect under the t-shirt, but for some reason that just annoyed me. Her expression was a hissing cat's, but she was too thrown to do much about it.

Still, the parking lot was lighted, if half-heartedly, and my actions were right out there for the world to see. Several patrons, groups of guys, a couple of couples, some girl duos, were laughing and making their way toward the Lucky from their various cars, but nobody thought twice about some jackass dragging a protesting girl along. Again, just that kind of town. . . .

"You *fucker!*" she said, her upper lip curling back. "You're in *trouble!*"

We were to the car now, and she started to scream, and I slapped her. The sound rang in the open air like a gunshot. She gave me a look that wondered how I could be such a brute to a beautiful girl like her.

"Shut up," I told her. "I'd rather kill you than fuck you."

She had a hand to her red-blossoming cheek, but that statement crinkled her forehead as her brain tried to process it.

I had her wrist in one hand and used my other to work the key in the trunk. The lid opened and I nodded toward the yawning space.

"Get in," I said.

"Fuck you," she said. But quietly.

"We need to talk, but here is not good. I won't hurt you if you behave. Get in."

By the way, I'd driven the Sunbird over to River Bluff on Wednesday, to give it a thorough cleaning, not that it would have fooled any forensics experts. But at least it wasn't blood-crustedly awful in there. I'm not that big a monster.

Anyway, she was crawling in, frowning, but more confused than afraid, when a hand grabbed my arm, and it was the bearded bouncer.

"*That's* not nice," he said, and head-butted me.

If I'd had the time for a thought, it would have been: *This is what happens, going around unarmed.*

But I didn't have the time.

When I woke up, I was lying on my back and looking up at ceiling tile.

"Little early for the game, aren't you, Jack?"

I knew the voice: Jerry G's.

And by now I knew where I was — supine, with my knees up, on one of the room-length built-in couches in the Lucky Devil's private poker room with its cream-color carpeted floor and walls. I could feel the

193

adhesive strip across my mouth, and more of it was around my wrists — silver duct tape — and more yet around my ankles above my running shoes.

"Only it isn't 'Jack,' is it? It's Quarry. What kind of name is that? Some kind of hired gun, aren't you? Working for Needle-Dickie Cornell?"

I didn't answer, because I couldn't. Anyway, these were rhetorical questions, or at least ones that Jerry G already knew the answers to: his little yellow-permed spy with the red Firebird had told him.

Most conversations between Cornell and me that might have been heard by Chrissy in part, or even in whole, had been somewhat elliptical. Only that had changed this evening with our most recent conversation, which had spelled it out so well that Jerry G didn't need to hear about it from me.

And, of course, Chrissy's spying ways explained how Jerry G had known I was an interloper at the Lucky Devil, a Cornell infiltrator at his card game, and arranged to have me beaten and maybe killed, if my mobile-home angel hadn't come along to save my ass.

Somehow I didn't think she'd come flying in to whisk me to safety this time.

Jerry G and I were not alone in the room.

Two bouncers were also present — the big bald black guy, and the bearded bruiser who had head-butted me. The black guy had an automatic stuffed in his waistband — a nine millimeter, I thought, but not a Browning like mine. Smith and Wesson maybe. The bearded guy had a Mad Max-style sawed-off shotgun in one beefy fist. He had too much belly for a gun to fit in his belt. Did I mention he was wearing amber goggle-type sunglasses? In fucking doors? Should be a capital crime.

As for my host, in a gray silk jacket over a black t-shirt with gold-chain necklaces and stonewashed blue jeans, he didn't appear to be armed — the jacket was open and no weapon showed in his waistband, nor any telltale bulge under either arm.

So all I had to deal with were a measly nine mil and a sawed-off. And a couple yards of duct tape. Piece of cake.

"You don't look the part," Jerry G said.

His horsey features had a dreamy cast, and I figured this was as philosophical a soliloquy as I could ever expect from him, even if I'd had a future.

He was saying, "You don't look tough. You don't seem like a psycho. Maybe that's how you stayed alive this long. But you know what they say — all good things must come to an end, you motherfucking prick."

He brought his elbow down into my nuts, like a wrestler faking a nasty blow, the kind that misses and jolts the canvas, only he wasn't faking and he didn't miss.

The pain was so intense, I saw flashing red and yellow stars, not cute cartoon ones, rather exploding ruptures, like the Fourth of July going off inside your skull. I'd heard Jerry G was a hothead, but he hadn't shown that side to me, leaving it to his boys to teach me that lesson in the alley the other day.

This, however, was over the line. He knew damned well this was just business. Put a bullet in my head and be done with it. But there's no reason, no excuse really, to lose your temper, and turn sadistic asshole. Unprofessional. Uncool.

"Cover this shit up," he was saying. "Dump his sorry ass."

I could see the carpeted room fairly well — Chrissy wasn't there, just Jerry G and his two bully boys. But on the floor was a canvas tarp, and the black guy reached for it, and that's what they were going to cover me up with.

But first the black guy swung the walnut-grip butt of his nine millimeter at my head. The angle was weird, and he couldn't put

196

much swing into it, and in that half-second or so, I figured it probably wouldn't kill me, but likely would put me to sleep.

It did.

When I came to, I was under the tarp on a metal surface and I could hear a raspy rumble, and feel the lurch and bounce and sway of what I quickly realized was a motorboat cutting through somewhat rough waters.

I got my bearings. I was in the bottom of the boat. My head was toward the stern, where the motor was grinding up foam at a pretty good clip. Twenty miles an hour? I was on my side, so my duct-taped hands were against the deck, which was steel and gently curved, nothing fancy — a jon boat?

I minimized my movement, but the tarp was so heavy, and the boat's trajectory loping enough, the engine noisy enough, that I figured I needn't worry too much. The tape looped around my hands put them in a praying position, but I hadn't stooped to prayer just yet. I still had better options.

And the best one was to find something sharp enough to work at the duct tape. These guys weren't the brightest, or maybe their boss Jerry G wasn't, because if they'd used any kind of rope, I really *would* have been praying — and making every promise to the Man Upstairs you can think of, about my new reformed life. As it was, they'd used duct tape.

And duct tape is *designed* to tear easily.

"River's a rough fucker tonight," a high-pitched, whiny voice said from the bow.

"Pretty, though," came a more mellow, lower-pitched voice from nearer me, at the stern, working itself above the motor. "Nice clear night, for so choppy."

This was the black guy, I'd venture. He had a soothing bass, with an Isaac Hayes vibe to it. The asshole at the bow was clearly white, probably the bearded head-butt artist with the beer belly.

"Wish to fuck I'd brought a jacket," the white guy said.

"You got that right."

"Is that why the river's so empty? Too fuckin' cold?"

"Yeah. Normally, this time of year, even this time of night? You'd have *some* assholes out drinkin' and drownin'."

"There was a few up nearer River Bluff."

"Yeah. They'll be more down Ft. Madison way."

The river seemed to settle down a little. I wished they would start talking again. I'd thought the way my wrists were bound, I might be able to get my fingers down to where I could get enough purchase to do some judicious ripping. But that wasn't happening. So now I was trying to explore the bottom of the boat, and find something sharp to work the duct tape on.

Two or three minutes went by before the white guy blurted: "Will you look at that full the fuck moon! Not a goddamned cloud in the sky. *Look* at them fuckin' stars! . . . Ever wonder if anybody's up there lookin' back down at us?"

"What, like God, you mean?"

"Naw, not Jesus or nobody. I mean, outer-space-type aliens. You know, *Star Trek* shit. E.T. phone the fuck home?"

The black guy chuckled. "I don't think so."

"What, so then, like, we're all *alone* down here? Whole great big universal galaxy, and it's just us idjits? I mean, what are the fuckin' *odds?*"

"Odds, one hunnerd percent."

"How you figure?"

"One hunnerd percent, fool. Ain't no aliens on a star."

"And why is *that,* smart-ass?"

"Because a star is a gaseous mass."

The white guy made a farting sound with his lips. "*You're* a gaseous mass."

"Maybe so. But I ain't a ignorant *redneck* gaseous mass."

That shut the white guy up.

I was enjoying the conversation — not because of its intellectual aspects, or its rustic American humor, but liking that these two stupid sons of bitches were distracting each other, while I was moving my hands down to where the metal hooks for a middle bench would've been, had it not been removed so the boat could be used for hauling contraband and dumping bodies and other fun and games.

I damn near laughed — the black guy on a bench at the stern, the bearded idiot on a bench at the bow, and me in the middle again. Didn't take long at all, and made zero noise (at least any that registered), using the metal edge of that fastener to carve through the duct tape.

The white guy asked, "Where should we dump the cocksucker?"

"Let's give it another ten miles or so."

"*Before* Ft. Madison, though."

"Yeah. Before."

". . . You know, my brother's in there."

"Huh? Where?"

"Ft. Madison! The pen!"

"What's he in for?"

"Killed a dude at a register, 7-Eleven."

"That was stupid."

"Well, the dude had a gun under there. That's self-defense!"

The black guy had no comment.

I had removed the duct tape from my mouth, for comfort, not practicality, but had decided that I could not risk undoing the tape locking my ankles — that would likely create obvious movement under the tarp.

"Somethin' about me," the white guy was saying, as they spoke across my prone form, "might surprise your black ass."

"Such as?"

"I like that soul music."

"You do, huh?"

"I ain't no redneck. That's racial. You shouldn't say that kind of racial shit."

"Yeah. Sorry. So. What do you listen to? Otis? Wicked Pickett? Aretha maybe?"

"Who? No, no! I like them *Blues* Brothers."

". . . You gotta be fuckin' *shittin'* me. . . ."

"What?"

"Them pasty white boys can't sing that shit."

"Hell they can't!" Then he started singing "Soul Man," which I thought was pretty funny, though I didn't laugh, too busy taking a chance lifting the edge of the tarp near my head just enough to get a fix on where the black guy was. . . .

The black guy, who told the white guy to shut the fuck up — which only made the bastard sing louder, intermingling it with laughter — was wearing gray running shoes. Big ones — size elevens, anyway, with some miles on them. I got a good look, because those stompers were about five inches from the edge of the tarp.

Then the white guy started singing "Rubber Biscuits," and this the black guy found funny as hell, lightening up, and he was laughing right up until my hands gripped his ankles and brought him sliding down hard onto the floor of the boat, rocking the little craft.

I stood up, like a ghost waking, and flung the tarp off and at the bearded bouncer at the stern, getting a glimpse of the sawed-off, which wasn't in his hands, rather down in the floor of the boat, a nice break for me.

The black bouncer, whose nine mil was still in his waistband, had let go of the stick guiding the motor (and the boat), which now ran sort of on automatic pilot. He was fumbling not for the gun but for something to push up on, so he could get on his feet and deal with me. He was also saying, *"Fuck!"* over and over again.

The guy was big all right, but right now

he was just a bug on its back, and I didn't have that much trouble shoving him over the side, rolling him off; he made a smaller splash than you'd think, and — on my knees on the metal floor — I grabbed for the stick and swung the boat hard left, sending the bearded guy, still tangled in the tarp, over the right side (the dope still had the amber sunglasses on — at night!), and a hand that had just got hold of the sawed-off lost its grip, leaving the weapon behind.

As the boat swung around, the triple rotors of the Evinrude 25 HP came in contact with the black guy, who was splashing around and treading water desperately. The blades sheared his face off and a noseless red mask remained; as his screaming split the night, I swung the boat around in a circle and the bearded fucker managed to swim just out of its path, but his scarlet-masked partner got another helping, hands coming up protectively and fingers flying like sausages. Somewhere along the line, a rotor blade must have caught his neck, because a geyser of red headed for the moon and didn't make it.

The bearded guy was still swimming away from me — I had straightened the craft around — but he hadn't got very far, not far enough to avoid the sawed-off's blast, which exploded his head and those stupid goggles with it and left him with his neck making its own fountain, not that the moon was ever in any danger of stain.

Then they were both bobbing there, with the night nicely quiet, the river otherwise empty, the full moon giving the water an ivory sheen. The gaseous masses of the universal galaxy made reflections, except where the river had gone frothy with reddish foam.

I headed upstream. Never had much experience with motorboats, but I was getting the hang of it.

ELEVEN

On the trip upriver, I grew increasingly uncomfortable in the cold. Some dark clouds had started rolling in, smudging the moon, a wind kicking up, making the water even choppier. I was in a short-sleeve shirt and all I had to put over me was that fucking tarp, and that wasn't going to happen. But it was good for my head, the chill, because I could think with more clarity.

I was missing my wallet, but that was no big deal — nothing in it but some fake John B. Gibson I.D., driver's license, social security, a couple of credit cards. The money from the poker game that I'd woken up with on me was not an issue — I'd stowed it in my suitcase back at the motel, after leaving Candace's mobile home and before going to see Cornell at the Paddlewheel. And speaking of the motel, I still had my room key, stuffed deep in my right front pocket.

Also, I'd been left my wristwatch, which was nothing expensive, just a Timex, and yes the sucker was still ticking — it was ten after midnight. Tonight's poker game at the Lucky Devil hadn't even started yet.

I'd given thought to pulling the jon boat in at the Paddlewheel's little dock, but my Sunbird was in the Lucky Devil lot, and I decided to see if I could risk docking at Jerry G's landing. That pier was more elaborate than the Paddlewheel's, with a few other jon boats tied up, plus a brick boathouse for the cabin cruisers that were part of the "recreational boating" fleet that was actually used for drug-, gun-, and who-the-fuck-knew-running.

Fairly adept with the Evinrude by now — my little outing with the two bouncers had taken me maybe twenty miles downriver — I slowed and had a look at the dock, where the only lighting was one yellow security lamp on the boathouse itself. I could see nobody standing watch, the jon boats bobbing at an empty expanse of pier. I glided in and tied up there, and crawled up on the spongy dock.

I had no weapon other than the sawed-off, and I'd used one of its two shells — any reloads had gone down with its previous owner. But it was a formidable-looking weapon and I could still do one blast's worth of damage, so it was worth hauling along.

A gravel path wider than a sidewalk and narrower than a one-lane road made its way up the slope through trees to the edge of the Lucky Devil parking lot, which was full now. Post-midnight Friday was prime time for the Lucky. The security lighting was subdued, with the handful of lamp poles outshone by the occasionally opening doors of the hooker trailers lining the lot at right and left.

I moved toward where I'd left the Sunbird, with the sawed-off at my side, staying close to cars so that the weapon couldn't be easily seen. Parking places were rare enough that arriving vehicles were trolling for them, and when a car found a space, it swung in to disgorge drivers and passengers who had already long since passed any legal drinking limit. Dumb loud remarks and drunken louder laughter made dissonant music in the open air.

When I got to where I'd left the Sunbird, I at first thought I'd miscalculated, and was off a row, because the Pontiac wasn't there. Then I leaned against the Dodge in its space and thought it through: my car keys hadn't been on me, so that meant Jerry G's minions had located the Sunbird and moved it, dumped it somewhere.

You're a dead man, I reminded myself. *They couldn't have left your wheels just hanging around their parking lot. . . .*

Up a row, however, another Pontiac caught my attention — a familiar cherry-red vehicle that was still in its place: Chrissy's Firebird convertible, with the top down.

I was maybe twenty feet from the building now, so I lowered my head as I made my way to the Firebird, then knelt beside it, and got the lay of the land. A single bouncer, situated near the casino, was walking the line, keeping an eye on the lot. He didn't seem to have spotted me, and his only brothers were walking the perimeters where the hooker trailers perched.

Three bodyguards, then . . . with the ones babysitting the hookers way too busy to be overly bothered with the parking lot.

I hadn't expected to see any increased security — after all, had everything gone peachy for the boys dumping me downriver, they would just be getting back. They might not even be expected to check in with the boss, who soon would be playing his precious poker game, and disliked being interrupted.

Speaking of which, after I'd kept watch

for possibly fifteen minutes, the door to the private poker room abruptly opened, and a familiar yellow-permed figure exited, with Jerry G following her a step or two. They exchanged a few words, he patted the behind of her tight jeans, then slipped back inside as she started toward the lot.

I hopped in the back of the convertible, and positioned myself on the floor behind the front seats. The Firebird was parked about mid-lot, which was its most under-lit section, and I figured I could get away with it. Anyway, I didn't suppose Chrissy felt she needed any weapon that God hadn't already granted her, but if she'd upgraded to a revolver or something, and had it handy in her pink purse, I had a shotgun shell available to rearrange her perm.

She got in the car and behind the wheel, started it up, and pulled out, wheels crunching gravel and then I felt the shift onto the smooth blacktop of Main Street. That was when I slipped the double-nose of the shotgun between the seats and into her bare side — I was still tucked below sight of anybody but birds and truckers.

"Jesus!" she said, and hit the brakes.

"Keep driving," I said.

She tried to see me in her rear-view mirror, but the angle was wrong. "What?"

"It's your Coke buddy. I'm not dead. But you will be, if you fuck around."

"I'm not *afraid* of you!" she said, terrified. "What if I go one hundred miles an hour and crash us?"

"Then we'd both be dead, only I won't let you take this baby past forty-five, without reducing your waistline first."

I poked her flesh with the shotgun's cold snout.

"You . . . you wouldn't shoot me. . . ."

"I think I would. Drive us to the Wheelhouse Motel. Pull in the space at room twenty-eight."

A maybe three-minute drive followed, proving as uneventful as it was silent. I felt the car slide into the stall, and she shut the car off.

"Now what?" Her voice sounded entirely different, sort of medium-range, that middle ground between alto and soprano, and grown-up. Before, all she'd emitted was a sullen, childish mumble. I realized these last few minutes were the first time I'd heard her speak when she wasn't bored, or pretending to be, anyway.

I hopped out of the back, facing the room, the shotgun in front me, out of sight from any motel guests who might have been loitering, although there really weren't any

210

— they were all around the bend down at the Paddlewheel.

"Get out," I told her.

She gazed up at me in fear and loathing — she looked a little like Tuesday Weld, *Dobie Gillis*-era, though her cheeks were more sunken; still, it was Tuesday's smirky kiss of a mouth. Her eyes, dark blue and large, showed no sign she'd been tooting recently, neither dilated nor red. She'd apparently spent her time with Jerry G in the private poker room either filling him in or getting filled by him. Or both.

I unlocked the room and she went in first, and sat on the edge of the bed, still in thc pink shirt tied under her nice little titties, her jeans so tight they would have given Brooke Shields pause. The pink purse was beside her, and I reached over and flipped it out of her reach.

She was studying me. Looking to see how much trouble she was in. Looking to see how she could get out of it.

I went to my suitcase on its stand and got out my spare nine millimeter, and left the sawed-off on top of some clothes.

"Let me tell you all about you," I said, pulling up a chair opposite where she sat, but angling it so my back wouldn't be entirely to the door.

"You don't know me," she said.

"You were a cheerleader in high school, but you had a bad reputation, well-deserved. Your grades and activities were just good enough to get you into college, but you either flunked out or got in trouble over drugs, and so you started dancing. Maybe in Chicago. You caught somebody's eye in family circles, maybe Jerry G himself, on a visit . . . but anyway, when Jerry G *did* see you, he knew you were something special, way too cute to waste on dancing or whoring, and anyway you didn't like to think of yourself as a whore, so you became Jerry G's favorite little squeeze. He lavished you with credit cards and cocaine, with never a notion of wasting you in any capacity at the Lucky, and then he got an idea. He knew all about Dickie Cornell's weaknesses, and he needed somebody to keep an eye on the Brit prick's activities and ambitions. So you enrolled in community college in River Bluff . . . probably just a class or two . . . and you applied as a waitress at the Paddlewheel. I've seen the female help there, it's like walking around inside a men's magazine. But you are exceptionally cute, Chrissy, even by Paddlewheel standards, and when Dickie interviewed you, you two hit it off. Were you ever a waitress there, I wonder, or maybe a bartender? Or was it straight up to the *Playboy* penthouse on the third floor, with hot-and-cold running tootski and all the decadence a nice Midwestern girl could ever dream of?"

She had started frowning about halfway through that. The frown indicated that in about ten years she'd look like hell, even if at the moment she did look heavenly.

She said, "You didn't get everything right."

"What did I miss?"

She didn't say anything.

"Come on," I prompted her. "What did I get wrong?"

"I wasn't a cheerleader. I was a pom-pom girl."

"Even better."

"And I *never* danced. I was never a fucking . . . *stripper.*"

I could see that. Her boobs were even smaller than Candace's.

"What *were* you, then?"

"I was a hostess at a restaurant."

"An Italian restaurant?"

"Yes, an Italian restaurant! What of it? . . . Listen, I haven't broken any laws or anything."

"You haven't? When did cocaine get legalized? While I was away on a boat trip?"

"I mean, it's not illegal to fool somebody.

213

Or to tell somebody else about somebody else."

"You mean, not illegal to work for Jerry G and spy on Dickie Cornell? You could be right, but when you're dealing with men whose business is illegal gambling, or in Jerry G's case, gambling and prostitution and drug-running, legal doesn't come into it. Somebody feels fucked over, so somebody else . . . somebody like *you,* for example . . . gets killed."

Her chin came up. Her defiance was almost equal to her fear. "Are you going to kill me?"

"I don't think so. You almost got *me* killed, though, tonight, so it's a possibility."

Her eyes and nostrils flared. "How did I get you . . . almost get you . . . killed?"

"You told Jerry G about the conversation you overheard today — about me 'taking care of' Jerry G for Dickie bird. And then Jerry G handed me over to a couple of pals of his, who took me for what was supposed to be a one-way boat ride."

The big blue eyes went to half-mast. "I don't know what you're talking about."

"I don't know if you do. I don't know if I care. Tell me, what's on Jerry G's mind tonight?"

She blinked; nice long lashes, under the

214

mascara. "On his mind?"

"Yeah. You just came out of that private poker den of his. What's his mood?"

"Well . . . good, I guess. Just getting ready for his regular Friday night poker game."

"Didn't seem anxious? Waiting for word on some pressing matter?"

"No. He was in a good mood."

This was encouraging. He clearly felt I was out of the picture. No extra security measures were being put into motion at the Lucky, meaning no reason to think I'd be up against anything out of the ordinary. The only possible hitch was if he expected to hear from the boys in the boat.

But why *should* they report back? As far as Jerry G was concerned, I was a dead man. They were just out dumping the garbage. They'd probably either go home or resume their duties at the club, and with as many bouncers as Jerry G employed, on a busy Friday night, the pair might not be missed.

I hoped I wasn't kidding myself.

"That Firebird," I said. "Is it yours?"

"Yes."

"You make payments on it?"

"No. It was a gift."

"From Jerry G?"

"Actually, from a nice man in Chicago

215

who's a friend of Jerry G's."

I frowned at her. "A man named Giardelli? *Vince* Giardelli?"

". . . Yes."

Vince was Jerry G's godfather, just as Tony was Cornell's, courtesy of wife Angela. That meant the insertion of Chrissy as an under-the-covers agent at the Paddlewheel was a scheme conceived at the highest lowlife level.

I said, "The Firebird — where do you keep the title?"

"Well, in my glove compartment. Where else?"

Oh, a safe deposit box maybe, or a fire-proof safe. But somehow I knew Chrissy would come through for me, with just the right idiocy.

"I need wheels," I said. "Jerry G stole my car and dumped it somewhere. I'll buy it from you. I'll give you cash, and you'll sign the title over."

"I don't want to sell it."

"I wasn't asking. I'll give you four grand."

"It's worth a lot more!"

"I know it is, but because of you, the other day I got beaten to that bloody pulp you hear so much about, and then, this evening, almost got killed and dumped in the Mis-sissippi. So I figure you owe me. Anyway, you know what they say — you lose half the value the minute you drive it off the lot."

She thought she understood me now. She unknotted the pink shirt and let the twins out for some air. They were small but perfectly shaped and tilted up, and the nipples were large and puffy and very appealing.

"I told you before," I said, "that I'd rather kill you than fuck you."

The little Tuesday Weld mouth was twisting into a knowing one-sided smile. "I don't think so."

She stood. Kicked off the sandals. Unzipped the jeans, tugged them off, and as tight as they were, that was fascinating to watch. The jeans left some marks, but nothing that detracted. She had no underpants on, and her pubic triangle was just as yellow as her hair — I was pretty sure she dyed it, and the bush had been cut into a heart shape and thinned a little. Very stylish, and thoughtful, coming from such a self-centered brat.

You must have a very low opinion of me to think I'd fall for this game. That this detestable little cunt could seduce me so easily. For one thing, I didn't have a rubber handy, and I wasn't sticking an arrow into *that* heart unprotected — that reckless I'm not. And for another, she was a detestable little cunt . . . or did I say that?

I did let her blow me, though, and she was good, very thorough and skilled and while I wouldn't say she enjoyed herself, she seemed to take a certain pride in her work. When she was done, cheeks less sunken, containing a mouthful of me now, she held up a "wait" finger, and padded naked into the bathroom, where she spit it out in the john, flushed it, then went to the sink and partook of my mouthwash.

"You can use my toothbrush if you want," I called. Gracious host that I am.

"Thanks!"

"It's still only four grand for the car."

The water was running. Wasn't sure she heard me.

I got on the phone. The desk at the Wheelhouse was open all night.

"You folks have any clothesline or rope up there?" I asked.

"No, Mr. Gibson. Sorry."

"Damn. Well . . . how about duct tape?"

By dawn, the parking lot at the Lucky Devil was almost empty. I supposed Chrissy's red Firebird was a little conspicuous among all those absences, but on the other hand, it was a familiar set of wheels here. I parked back almost to the trees and sat and watched.

The hookers began exiting their trailers with little suitcases, heading for home. After spending fifteen minutes checking his watch every three, the parking lot bouncer went in the casino exit, off-duty apparently. Some dancers and waitresses came for their cars, which were also parked toward the back, leaving me more bare than a Lucky Devil stripper at the end of her third song.

I had the dark-blue windbreaker on over a light-blue polo shirt; also black jeans and running shoes. Also the nine millimeter, in my right hand, in my lap.

At a little after six, Jerry G — still in the gray silk suit and black t-shirt and gold chains — escorted some guests out the exit of the private poker room, nobody I recognized from the mid-week game. They had the well-dressed look and confident bearing of the high-stakes player, though they were dragging some, having played all night. And some, presumably, had lost some dough.

Then Jerry G stepped back in and closed the door.

I stuffed the nine millimeter in my waistband, got out of the Firebird and headed quickly toward the building. I had my right hand on the butt of the nine mil when I knocked with my left on the poker-room door, not a minute after the last guest had gone.

Jerry G opened the door, initially with a pleasant, curious expression that shifted to shock, then rage, then fear, as I pushed through and shut the door behind me.

I'd been hopeful the room would be empty but for Jerry G, knowing I might face the problem of a lingering guest and/or a barmaid tidying up. And I caught a break — it was just Jerry G and me.

I pushed him toward the table, not rough, not gentle.

"Sit," I said.

He took his usual dealer's seat, shaking his head. "Where are Bubba and Bruno? What the hell did you do to them?"

"That redneck went by Bubba? Really?"

He didn't answer. His horsey face was as pale as dead skin. Even his Frankie Avalon pompadour seemed a little droopy. "You . . . you *killed* them?"

"I think it was the motorboat engine props that killed Bruno, assuming you mean that big black bastard. Took his face off, like a slice of meat from an Oscar Mayer loaf, and some fingers, too. And it caught him in the throat. Bubba, assuming that's the white prick? Him I killed, with the sawed-off he would've used on me."

"My God . . . where . . . where did you leave them?"

"Where do you think? They're floating. Your chums are chum."

That was a little cute. But I was pretty hyper, so cut me some slack. I was pissed at this guy, otherwise I'd have shot him by now.

"What was the idea," I said, "of that elbow in the nuts? What did I ever do to you?"

"Are you . . . are you kidding? You came here to *kill* me, didn't you?"

"No, *first* I was trying to figure out if you were the one who hired somebody to kill Cornell. You might have got a pass. But now I just don't care."

Hope and fear flickered in his eyes, as if fighting for control. "I'll pay you *twice* what he is. What's he paying you? I'll give three *times!*"

"Not an option. Conflict of interest kind of deal."

His eyes showed the white all around now. "*Listen* to me, Quarry . . . you can walk out of this room a rich man — I can have half a million deposited wherever you say, Swiss account, Caymans, you name it."

I lifted the hand that wasn't training a gun on him. "No, you see, you'd hold a grudge. You'd give me the money, sure . . . but then people would come try to kill me, and that would take the fun out of it."

He had both his hands up, his palms out — surrendering, in a way; but still trying, as he said, "What can I do to make this right?"

"Nothing," I said. "But I do want to thank you for one thing."

". . . *What* the fuck?"

"Soundproofing this room."

I put one in his forehead, and his skull didn't explode exactly, but it definitely cracked, and after he'd gone backward initially, he flopped forward on the table and spilled blood and brains on the green felt.

I didn't leave immediately — I had noticed his little tin box on the bar, which held the bank from the recent poker game. Taking a quick look, I determined Jerry G had done very well tonight — the box had twenty grand in it. Make a lucky devil joke here, if you're so inclined.

The tin box of money I tucked under my left arm, and — with the nine millimeter in my hand, and my hand in the right pocket of my windbreaker — strolled out into the dead parking lot and got into my new car.

TWELVE

The morning had stayed chill, the sky smoky gray. One of those cold days in Hell they always talk about, or anyway a cold day in Haydee's.

It was six-thirty-something when I pulled into the Paddlewheel lot, which was empty save for two cars, one of them Richard Cornell's Corvette, the other Angela Dell's little red Subaru. I'd figured there was a good chance everybody would be gone for the night/day, except for Cornell himself, and I was almost right — and the only other person still here was part of the family, in a couple senses.

So my timing was excellent, particularly considering that my client — typically spiffy in a navy blazer, yellow sport shirt and light-blue trousers — was exiting the big old reconverted warehouse and striding toward his Corvette, parked toward the rear of the lot. Had I been Monahan doing his vehicular homicide bit, I'd have been in perfect position to send Dickie flying into the next life or at least a hole in the ground.

But of course I'd turned down Jerry G's offer for a contract on my boss, for reasons previously stated.

He saw the Firebird pulling in, and smiled, thinking it was Chrissy come to see him, which was sort of true. Then he made me behind the wheel and frowned, not in displeasure, just confusion. I stopped next to him and got out. He met me at the rear of the sporty red convertible.

"Something I want to show you," I said.

The white crease lines formed in the too-tanned forehead. "What are you up to, love?"

"This is sort of where I came in," I said, and unlocked the trunk.

The lid popped up to reveal, down in the well, the little yellow-permed Chrissy in her pink blouse (unknotted and loose now) and tight jeans and sandals, on her side fetally, front of her toward us as she craned her head to glare at me, the big dark-blue eyes popping over the wide slash of silver duct tape. She tried to call me something but I couldn't quite make it out, though I think I got the gist.

I'd taped her wrists behind her and

wrapped the stuff all over and around her little fists, in hopes that would keep her bound. Her ankles were taped tight, too. She didn't seem to have budged, which either meant she wasn't as ambitious or smart as I'd been on that boat, or maybe I had just done a better job of taping her up.

Cornell's yap was hanging open. "What the bloody *hell . . . ?*"

I shut the trunk, and took him by the elbow, walking him near the line of trees at that end of the lot.

"Little girls have big ears," I said, keeping my voice low and raising a shush finger.

"I didn't hire you to kill some innocent —"

"First of all, she's about as innocent as Marilyn Chambers, and second, she's still breathing. And I'm not going to make her stop, either. You can do what you want with her, from spank her to toss her dead in a ditch, but it's not a job I want."

I quickly explained that Chrissy had been Jerry G's industrial espionage agent, and Cornell found this news predictably dismaying.

"I thought I was a better judge of character than that," he said, shaking his head, the half-lidded, unblinking aqua eyes taking on a hurt, almost haunted quality.

"Dickie, you may be a good judge of character, but few heterosexual males are good judges of character when that character is attached to a tight little twenty-year-old pussy. If you'll pardon my bluntness. Anyway, the job is done and maybe we can transfer that package to your trunk, and you can do whatever the fuck you —"

"*What* job is done?"

"Are you kidding? Jerry G is still warm but *he's* not breathing."

". . . You did it. You really did it."

"What did you think I was going to do? Performance art?"

"I mean . . . before, it seemed *abstract.* . . ."

"That other body in the trunk I showed you, that seemed abstract to you?"

He was going pale despite the tan. "How . . . how did it go down?"

"I told you I don't do details. How it's perceived depends on Jerry G's Chicago partners and the bent local cops. It'll probably be one of two ways — a robbery/homicide, or a boating accident. Or even, with the right doctor, natural causes. My guess is, the last thing Jerry G's associates want, and I include both Chicago and the county sheriff's department, is a homicide that brings in state cops. That kind of investigation could shut down Haydee's Port, you included, at least for a while."

He didn't contradict me. He seemed in shock.

"What should I do with her?" he said finally, nodding toward the trunk.

"I wouldn't kill her."

"*Jesus!* Neither would I!"

"Give her a second chance. Maybe make her work for her supper as a hostess or something. Or send her back to Chicago. She has friends there. Oh . . ." I got an envelope out of my windbreaker jacket pocket. The envelope came from the Wheelhouse Motel, and it was plump with hundred dollar bills — four grand worth. "Give this to Chrissy. I bought her car."

A sick slice of white appeared in the dark face — a smile, technically anyway. "A little flashy for you, isn't it, Quarry?"

"I don't know. Bright red car might be a nice souvenir of my trip to Haydee's. Or I might trade it in for something more suited to my part of the world."

"Where is that?"

"You don't really want to know."

"No. No, I don't. I wasn't thinking."

"Right. Now let's transfer the package from my trunk to yours. . . ."

He had no objection, and I was about to

pop the lid when someone exited the big brick building — a woman, and we were far enough away that Cornell felt he had to prompt me.

"That's just Angie," he said.

But I already knew that, because I'd made her car. His wife or ex-wife or whatever she was strolled right toward us, which was natural, because she belonged to the one remaining ride in the lot. She was wearing jeans, rather looser than those Chrissy preferred, and a white blouse whose sleeves stopped at mid-forearm and with some ruffles up the front, like a gambler's shirt seen on a real paddlewheel a hundred years ago.

"Fellas," she said, with a smile. She looked her age in the cold morning light, with no lipstick and not even eyeshadow, but her face was nice enough to get away with it. Her red hair was pinned and piled up like a turban, nothing fashionable, just getting it out of her way. "This looks like a serious pow-wow."

"My friend Mr. Gibson has finished his work for me," Cornell said stiffly.

Angela — who not long ago had helped me dump two bodies (let's call it aiding and abedding) — knew damn well that that "work" almost certainly had to be something on the nasty side; but she didn't blink. She was, after all, this man's wife — separated or not — and moreover she was Tony Giardelli's daughter. She had spent a lifetime on the fringes of violence and had to be used to it, or at least used to ignoring it.

"Sorry to hear you're going, Jack," she said, and offered me her hand, and I shook it. She gave it a secret squeeze. "Kind of hoped we'd have time for that breakfast you promised me. I'm headed over to the Wheelhouse diner now. . . ."

"Grab a booth in back. I have to check out of my room. Before I hit the road, I could use a meal, wouldn't mind some pleasant company."

She said sure, smiled at me, nodded at her sort of husband, and went over to the Subaru and stirred gravel a little as she exited.

"What are you, hitting on my wife?" he asked, with an eyebrow arched.

"Maybe I already fucked her till eyes rolled back."

"You can be crude sometimes, Mr. Quarry."

"Normally no. Haydee's Port is a bad influence on me. It's all sex and murder and money, and an All-American boy like me can get corrupted. Shall we move the little slut?"

For now, we tucked Chrissy in his trunk, and she squirmed like a calf not wanting to get branded, making noises of protest that came off strangely like yummy sounds.

I left him there, standing at the rear of the Corvette, staring at the closed trunk. For a moment I wondered if he might not kill her, or have her killed, at that.

But it wasn't any of my business.

Angela Dell had taken the same booth we'd shared before, and of course she remained unaware that, a few days and several lifetimes ago, Monahan and the blond kid had sat there, too, and plotted her husband's death.

She was drinking coffee already, and when I joined her, I ordered iced tea. Coffee was for grown-ups. I was hugely hungry — I'd been through a lot of unappetizing shit over the past twenty-four hours or so, but hadn't eaten a thing since my mobile-home Florence Nightingale had fed me leftover alphabet soup.

So I ordered scrambled eggs, hash browns, link sausage and silver-dollar pancakes. She had a half order of French toast and we ate in silence for a while — well, not quite silence: a breakfast the size of mine, on a stomach that empty, required some spirited grunting and swallowing and silverware clanking.

She watched me with mild amusement, just nibbling at her French toast. When I pushed my cleaned plate aside, she said, "I don't know what to make of you."

"Nothing *to* make."

"What makes you tick, Jack?"

"Nothing. You're just hearing the Timex." I lifted my wrist. It got another little smile out of her. "I'm glad we had a chance to say goodbye, though."

"Me, too. Oh!" She had a big black purse with her, and she dug inside it, came back with a CD — on the cover was a photo of her in a low-cut dress, soft-focus, sultry, and I'd guess taken around 1960 or '61. She made Julie London look like a boy. It was called *Angela on Your Shoulder*.

"This is the Verve album you made," I said, smiling. "Will you sign it?"

"I already have. I . . . didn't use your name, since I know Jack isn't really it."

I popped the jewel case open and read what she had signed, in black felt-tip, across a song list of Rodgers and Hart, Cole Porter, Johnny Mercer and Frank Loesser: "To my favorite one-morning stand. Yours

231

always, Angie." Then, pro that she was, she had signed her full signature below: Angela Dell.

"This means a lot," I said. "I don't treasure much, but I'll treasure this."

"Least I could do."

"Probably, considering I didn't tell your husband you're the one who hired his murder."

She dropped her coffee cup, but it was mostly empty and didn't spill, didn't even break.

We had that section to ourselves, and our voices were low, so I wasn't making a scene. Her dropping the coffee cup was as close to making a scene as either of us came.

She said, her voice as throaty as if she were singing "Cry Me A River," "You can't be *serious,* Jack. . . ."

"Dead serious. Jerry G's father is so out of it, he gives senility a bad name — he couldn't organize a fart in the bathtub, let alone set up a hit. And as for Jerry G? He was going to the trouble of having Dickie spied on — baby Madonna, remember?"

"That . . . that girl *Chrissy?* She was working for Jerry G?"

"Yeah. Oh, he's dead, by the way. Somebody shot him about . . . not quite an hour ago. I believe it was a robbery, but it'll probably wind up officially some kind of tragic accident. Powers-that-be wouldn't want Haydee's Port to go to hell."

"Jerry G is dead?"

"I'm not going to repeat myself. Your husband or whatever the hell he is hired me to deal with Jerry G, and I did. He was also considering having the old boy taken out, till I gave him the latest medical update."

"Just because that girl was spying on —"

"You don't bother gathering intel on somebody you've already hired someone else to eliminate. Period. Anyway, look at his behavior — Jerry G knew, from Chrissy, that I was working for your husband . . . but if he knew or suspected I was here to take him out, he wouldn't simply have had me beaten up — he would have had me killed. Last night he *did* try to have me killed, after he heard enough from Chrissy to gather I probably *did* have a contract from Dickie to remove his ass. But Jerry G stupidly sent a couple of bouncers to deal with me, who were in over their heads, or anyway are now."

She said nothing. A waitress strolled over, filled Angela's coffee from a container in one hand, and my iced tea from a pitcher in the other. Then we were alone again, us and our freshened liquids.

"What makes you think," Angela said very quietly, looking at her wedding-ring-free hands, folded neatly near the coffee cup, steam rising from it like ghosts, "that *I* took out the contract?"

"No other candidate makes sense. You are still the wife, separated or not, and that puts you in a position to inherit everything. You are by birth a Giardelli, and female or not, would be in a good position to, first, utilize your connections to set up a hit, and second, take over the Paddlewheel with Chicago's blessing. With your show biz background and expertise, all those years in Vegas, who better to run the Paddlewheel and its expanded operation? Especially when riverboat gambling comes in, and everything gets more respectable. . . . Also, as a wife, you'd be more likely to have an accident staged than a simple drive-by hit. Hell, maybe there was double indemnity! Didn't work for Barbara Stanwyck, but that's just an old Hollywood movie, where crime doesn't pay. Anyway, I don't see Jerry G as the kind of guy who'd go to the trouble of disguising a killing as an automobile accident."

Her lips trembled a little. Her voice, too: "What if . . . what if I told you I love my husband. That I *still* love my husband."

"Wouldn't surprise me. Your motivation

may be greed, or it may be love or anyway the kind of love that curdles into hate when your guy gives you table scraps — say, like your little ongoing piano bar gig — at the same time he's taking various baby Madonnas upstairs to his *Playboy* pad, for a banquet. These kinds of things are complicated. Emotions."

The wide-set green eyes were as unblinking as her husband's. "Why did you . . . *take care* of Jerry G, if you knew he wasn't responsible for the contract on Richard?"

I shrugged. "Hey, I made it clear to Dickie that I had my doubts about Jerry G. I let him know that my services included trying to determine who took the contract out, and so on. But Dickie was convinced it was Jerry G. He wanted Jerry G gone, and I admit I developed a certain grudge against the guy myself, so I took the job. Did the job. End of story."

The eyes remained wide but the flesh around them was tightening. "End of . . ."

"I haven't told Dickie about you, or anyway my theory about you."

Now she frowned. The eyes finally narrowed, and fear was in them. "What are you *after?* What do you *want* from me?"

I lifted the CD. "This'll do. This is plenty."

". . . You're not telling Richard?"

"No. I did the job he hired me to do, and I'm out of here."

"How do you know I won't . . . won't go to my 'Chicago connections' and somehow make this happen some *other* way?"

"I don't. Do what you want. Fuck him. Kill him. Fuck him, then kill him. He's *your* husband. But I don't want a contract from either one of you. I've had my fill of Haydee's Port."

She had a clubbed baby seal expression, and just couldn't find any words. Hard to sing torch songs over breakfast.

"I'll enjoy this," I said, gesturing with the CD, "I really will. . . . I'll get the check."

I left her there to contemplate her future, and Dickie bird's, and went to my room and showered and shaved and changed my clothes and got my things and got the hell out.

I did make one stop on my way — that little mobile home with the rusting Mustang out front. I had a paper bag in my left hand, held in a choke hold, like a trick-or-treater protecting his candy hoard.

I went up the handful of wooden steps and knocked. Nothing. It took prolonged and increasingly insistent knocking to get a response, and I finally got the little kid. He opened the door fearlessly and glared up at me.

"Mommy's sleeping," he said, and started to shut the door.

I pushed in, shut the thing behind me and looked down at the tow-headed boy in the *Star Wars* pajamas. "Listen, kid — I don't care if your mom *is* home. Don't go just opening the door 'cause somebody's knocking. You don't know who it might be."

From the bedroom came her voice: *"Jack?"*

"Go watch TV, kid," I said.

He gave me a dirty look but followed instructions, and I tiptoed around the wooden train set to where she was receding into the bedroom. She was in a t-shirt and cotton panties, had no makeup on and her natural blonde hair was ponytailed back and she looked fucking great.

"I didn't think I'd see you again," she said, her voice indicating she was glad she'd been wrong.

"Listen, Candace. I'm on my way out of town. When you left the Lucky, was there any fuss going down?"

"No."

"What time did you walk home?"

"Around quarter to six."

So she'd been gone when I dropped by to see Jerry G.

"Well, you need to know something," I said. "There's going to be a change of management. Some bad shit went down not long ago, but you don't know anything about it."

"I don't?"

"No." I handed her the paper bag.

"What's this?"

"Fifteen grand."

"What!"

"Yours."

She held it in a choke hold just like I had. "Are you *kidding. . . . Why . . . ?*"

"Because you saved my life. That's just some crumbs that got spilled, and maybe they'll do you some good. Thing is, there was a robbery over there at the Lucky . . . this isn't *that* money, you have to believe me, you have to *trust* me. . . ."

Of course, it was that money.

"All right . . . I believe you, Jack. Are you saying this money is . . . mine?"

"Yours. Here's the conditions. You run that over to River Bluff and put it in a safe deposit box — don't open an account. A safe deposit box. Then you go back to dancing at the Lucky and keep your head down during the management change and maybe any kind of investigation . . . ."

"Police?"

"Maybe. I doubt it, but maybe. Anyway, don't throw any of that money around. Just do your job, shake your titties and booty and make some men happy. Live your little life, then in a month or two, if it's quiet, you quit, take your kid somewhere and put him in school and go to beauty college and get your life in gear."

"Jack . . . oh, Jack."

And she kissed me. There was sex in it, sure, and gratitude — you can get a hell of a kiss out of girl, when you give her a paper bag full of fifteen grand — but mostly it was sweet. Loving. A hint of maybe what my life could have been like if it hadn't gone to hell a long time before I came to Haydee's.

"I got to run," I said, and gave her a peck of a kiss.

I moved carefully through the little train yard, and the kid kept his eyes on the tube — *Sesame Street* again — and I was halfway to the Firebird when she called out to me.

"Jack!"

She was framed there in the door, t-shirt, white panties, all the pale creamy flesh a man could ever want, and blue eyes that hid no secrets except the new one.

"You're an *angel,* Jack. When they made

you, they broke the mold!"
Didn't they just?